A Fierce Devotion

A Fierce Devotion

LAURA FRANTZ

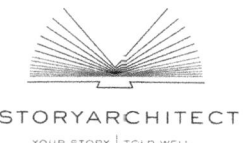

STORYARCHITECT

YOUR STORY | TOLD WELL

Who is that coming up from the wilderness,
leaning on her beloved?
Song of Songs 8:5

1

Western Virginia
1763

The damp May morning carried the earthy, hopeful scent of spring. Brielle stepped onto the porch of the *Rose and Crown* where, true to the tavern's name, an abundance of rose bushes crowded the stone exterior. About to bloom, they'd soon turn the air to perfume. Always first to wake, she felt a measure of peace in the dawn hush. Instead of bemoaning her five o'clock start, she tried to see it as less bane and more blessing. Doing so helped counter the darkness of her coming here and all the raw memories trailing behind it.

She hurried to the barn, the hem of her indigo petticoats drenched with dew. A striped barn cat meowed at her appearing, the open air exchanged for potent hay and manure and aged wood. She much preferred roses. Sitting down atop her milking stool, she spoke softly to the Devon cow she'd named *Fleur*. Streams of milk filled the freshly scrubbed bucket, muting Titus's approach as he passed through the barn.

At the ring of his ax, she nearly sighed aloud. At eight, he could split and stack wood like a man, his callused hands proof. He'd had no boyhood to speak of. Orphaned, his plight of being bound to the tavern's owner for seven more years made her ache when her own servitude was finished far sooner. What would become of him when she left?

What would become of *her*?

"Miss Brielle." The whisper came from the back of the barn.

Titus motioned for her to follow. Finished milking, she covered the full pail with a square of clean linen and toted it toward him and the milk house where an enormous elm shaded the cool space.

"Look here in this woodpecker hole." Titus smiled his lopsided smile, his split lip telling he'd been backhanded by their master. "A clutch of blue bird eggs—I count six."

Touched by the wonder in his tone, Brielle regarded the colorful eggs with genuine awe. "I forgive that old woodpecker for disturbing our sleep with his drumming, then."

Titus chuckled then sobered. "Hope that old coon lurking at our back door lately doesn't discover this nest."

"I pray not." She looked to the stables where she heard nickering and jostling, forgetting all about coons and birds. "Another lodger came in late last night."

"A post rider?"

"A scout."

"Trouble again?" His eyes rounded. "With French and Indians?"

"The Seven Years' War is over. The French have surrendered, remember."

If not the Indians.

She'd say no more lest she frighten him, moving on to churn the butter while he backtracked to the stables.

Midmorning had her clearing the tavern's public room. Breakfast had ended, the benches and long tables mostly empty. Across the wide main passageway was the bar serving ale and cider and other spirits from dawn till well past midnight. Rarely did she go there. The perpetually stale odor rankled though she was used to it. The barkeep was the surly Mr. Griffiths, the tavern's owner.

The scout she'd told Titus about sat near the bar's fireless hearth. He looked understandably weary, his expression as grim as he was gritty. She was used to that, too. She'd nearly forgotten Philadelphia where men and women dressed in fine garments and went about the city. Here there seemed nothing but humble farmers and frontiersman and their ilk.

"Miss Farrow, see that Ross is fed."

Brielle startled at Griffiths' voice. *Ross.* The scout? She gave a curt nod and swept past her bondsman into the kitchen where the tavern cook—the latest in a line of them—stirred something in a large kettle. Two of the enslaved helped her assemble a tray of fried venison, eggs, toast, and freshly ground coffee.

When she returned to the public room, Ross had left the bar and sat down at a just-cleared table. Eyes down, she served him silently, but that didn't discourage his conversation.

"You bound to Griffiths?" he murmured hoarsely.

She nodded, pouring coffee from a blisteringly hot pot.

"A shame."

She said nothing to this, fetching milk and sugar for his coffee. Griffiths might be a brute but he kept a respectable tavern. Folks came far and wide for the rarity of clean bed linens and cider from his orchards. But he didn't like her talking with his guests and so she mostly kept her eyes down and her mouth shut.

He took a stab at an egg. "Ever been proposed to?"

Flushing, she looked at him then and saw he was old enough to be her father. "Now and then."

He chuckled. "Bet you can't even count that high."

"I can't court nor marry without Mr. Griffiths' permission."

And he'd never give permission.

"Indentures are little better than slaves, at least while they're bound. How many years till you're free?"

"Two."

"Hope you get shed of here quicker than that. Griffiths is a hard man, disliked by many."

Lingering, she decided she'd risk Griffiths' ire to quell her curiosity. "What news do you bring?"

His affability vanished—and perhaps his appetite with it—as he set down his fork. "The backcountry is afire again. Several frontier forts are hard hit, fifteen killed near Tates Creek, and the bloodshed is spreading."

"Soldiers and settlers dead?"

"Settlers. A chief named Pontiac has rallied the tribes to fight back against all who take their lands. Virginia is rife with land stealers so the fight continues. I've come to carry a warning."

"You'll ride on to the back settlements."

"Of which this is one." The warning in his eye chilled her. Just west of the Blue Mountains and located near the northern entrance to the Shenandoah Valley, Brielle had often wondered what lay beyond the tavern at the crossroads.

He resumed his meal and she backtracked to the kitchen, trying to steady her nerves by the simple routine of washing the mound of breakfast dishes before working in the garden.

Frequent news of unrest and raids rumbled through the region. She knew the evils men were capable of though she'd rather not dwell on them. Just because they'd made peace with the French didn't mean they'd made peace with France's Indian allies. As long as British colonists continued to push west onto Indian lands there'd be unending conflict and blame.

Once Ross had breakfasted, he took to the tavern's front porch where settlement folk gathered to hear more details about the warning he'd given her earlier. His raised voice echoed back

4

to the kitchen garden behind the tavern and left her wishing she could close her ears.

By midafternoon the scout was on his way, his stabled horse brought round by Titus. The very air seemed charged with unrest. By suppertime more than travelers crowded the public rooms as settlers gathered to discuss bullet lead and fortifications and look-outs. The nearest fort—Loudoun—was several miles away, much too distant in time of attack.

As voices ebbed and flowed around her, Brielle served and refilled and cleared, her own stomach rumbling. Toward dusk she stood on the tavern's back stoop and looked westward where a skim of black smoke seemed to haze the sky. A burning cabin or barn? She studied the distant mountains, their clouded tops hazy. Something ominous twisted inside her and refused to budge.

Heavenly Father, preserve us, please.

2

*I*t was a mere jaunt of two hundred miles over the mountains, Bleu sometimes jested. Once he left Fort Pitt, he merely meandered along the Monongahela River then crossed the Allegheny Mountains with its steep ascents and descents before taking an Indian trail to enter the Shenandoah Valley. His sister—Sylvie—was east of that along the Rivanna River.

Oui, a mere jaunt.

The late spring weather was in his favor aside from a downpour or two. He wasn't the only one journeying through remote wilderness though one could go for days before seeing another living soul. He'd encountered plenty of dead ones. But that was during the last war when nothing had been safe nor sacred.

This trip his foremost concern was where to rest his horse and resupply himself along the way. He knew to avoid stops like *Bird-in-Hand* with its raucous patrons and bug-infested linens. Taverns like *The Red Fox* and *Rising Sun* he favored for their tidy, Virginia hospitality. Many a time he'd slept in some darkened stable when there'd been no beds, preferring horses to humans.

More than once he'd been mistaken for a traveling preacher with no home or tie to a place. On account of the Bible he carried, he guessed. Sometimes that rootlessness bedeviled him when a twinge in his joints reminded him he was older than thirty years. Or a missed meal told him he needn't miss any if he planted himself somewhere and made a home.

Home was no longer Acadie, lost to the British and renamed Nova Scotia. He tried not to think of that invasion and expulsion overlong. Eight years had passed since then, a blur of time spent as a guide, interpreter, and liaison between the tribes and colonies, often ending at the former Fort Duquesne, a remote garrison frequently fought over by the English and French. At the moment it was in English hands, having been wrested from the French and renamed Fort Pitt.

Hope and happenstance now found him on the move again in the North American wilderness as he came into the stump-littered clearing along the Red Fork River. In front of him stood Fort Randolph—or what was left of it. This had been the place of a massacre few had forgotten. Burnt during the last war, only the blockhouse stayed standing, a defiant outline in the dusk.

Further down the riverbank stood a log house. Light should have been flaring from Crown glass windows, a man standing on the front stoop shouting halloo but it was ransacked, too. Bleu felt a chill that had nothing to do with the spring damp. He walked through the ash and timber, looking for anything salvageable. It returned him unwillingly to Acadie when the British torched their homes and orchards and fields. Only this was the work of Indians. The signs were right.

Toward dusk when he'd pressed on another mile, he heard a rustle in the brush. Instinctively, his hand reached for the knife in his belt, suspecting an animal but finding a grizzled man staring back at him behind a sprawling laurel bush.

"Rest easy," the stranger said, straightening and relaxing his grip on his rifle. "You have the look of a hostile but something ain't quite right."

Bleu almost smiled. He'd been called worse. "Part Acadian, part Mi'kmaq. From Canada."

"Friend, not foe, then." The man ran a sleeve across his damp brow. He was so heavily bearded Bleu couldn't tell if he was young or old. The pronounced lump in his cheek foretold tobacco. "You're a far piece from the north territory."

"I quit Fort Pitt recently and am headed to the Rivanna River."

"I'm coming back from Cumberland country." He spat into the laurel. "And I'm done in. My horse threw a shoe about half a mile back but I remember a blacksmith being in the next settlement."

They made camp near a thin ribbon of creek away from the main trail. Dusk gathered with all its accompanying sounds and shadows as they talked in low tones. This man—Uriah Stone— was a Longhunter who knew the Virginia frontier well but had his sights on Tennessee and Kentucke.

"What news do you bring from Pitt?" he asked, passing jerked meat to Bleu. "Peaceable in that part of the country at long last?"

"Peaceable enough that Pitt's commandant is busy making a deer park and garden and bowling green instead of bullet lead— or was."

Stone chuckled then sobered. "Any truth to the rumor that Detroit's Indians are calling for uprisings up and down the frontier?"

Bleu nodded and swallowed the jerky. "The Seven Years' War may have ended for the British and French but no tribe will rest when overrun by the enemy and treaties are violated."

"So, what will you do once you reach the Rivanna?"

"Visit my sister and her family." Even now Bleu envisioned his nieces and nephews clamoring for attention, the youngest climbing his buckskin-clad legs like a tree.

Talbot, Amélie, Corbin, Madeleine, Morgan and Jolie.

By now Sylvie might have had another. His last visit was more than a year ago.

"What's the name?"

"Blackburn," Bleu replied.

"William Blackburn of Blackburn's Rangers?" Respect rode Stone's bearded features. "Started a settlement in central Virginia. Even wrote a book if I recollect rightly. And you?"

"I'm a former trader with Hudson's Bay Company turned scout and interpreter during the last war. As for the future, I'm at a crossroads."

"Maybe you could pen a book about your exploits like Blackburn."

Bleu shook his head. "My *histoire captivante* would fall far short of his."

"I beg to differ." Stone took a long drink from his flask. "I've heard tales of you Canadians and the like. Your Hudson's Bay adventures would fill more than one volume."

"I'd rather forget. Start afresh." Bleu took a drink from his own flask. "Canada holds a bitter taint."

"You wed?"

"Wedded to the wilderness." Would there ever be a *Madame* Galant? He doubted it. "And you?"

"Nay. Few women would put up with my tramps that last two years or better." He studied Bleu shrewdly. "I could use a hand with trapping and trading if you'd reconsider the Rivanna."

As a Longhunter? It held little appeal. He'd rather survey alongside his brother-in-law instead. Finish the house he'd begun in the foothills near his and Sylvie's home, Orchard Rest. Forge a different sort of life.

Perhaps even come to terms with all that had been lost.

"For now I need to see central Virginia. I've been away long enough my sister might be wondering if I'm still alive." Bleu looked through the trees where the sun was setting in a fiery show. "I may well tarry awhile this time. Nothing is more important than family. When you've lost much you treasure those who remain."

3

$\mathcal{M}$idnight brought stars so bright they seemed silver thread stitched into a black-silk sky, reminding Brielle of a gown worn by her mother long ago. She climbed to the attic up a back stair, her tiny room boasting a tinier window. On nights she wasn't too weary she liked to watch the moonrise, but tonight her very bones seemed to ache to say nothing of her heart.

Earlier, Griffiths in a drunken fury had taken a lash to Titus over some minor matter. Now the lad was so sore he could barely move. Brielle had gently bathed the back of his spindly legs then applied yarrow salve while a shaken Tamsen—Titus's sister—finished his evening chores. Afterwards, Titus and his sister retreated to their room opposite Brielle's beneath the attic's eaves. But pained as he was would he be able to sleep?

Once, early on, Griffiths had lashed her. Afterwards she'd been too bruised and bleeding to do her chores thus he'd not repeated it. She'd forgotten why he'd turned on her though the memory stayed sore. Titus's misery reminded her of it all over again.

Tonight, after washing at a basin on her windowsill, she lay down. Her treasured wash ball was nearly gone. A lodger had left it behind last winter and its clove scent seemed a gift given the harsh soft soap she herself made from lard and lye in late fall.

Tomorrow was the Sabbath when they could rest. The saddle-bag preacher would come and give a sermon on the tavern's front steps. He only came round once a month or so and most settlers who lived within riding or walking distance turned out to hear him preach. Some said he made hell so vivid one could find it on a map. Young and lined, the fearless Methodist rode round Virginia's back country in all seasons.

"*Mon Dieu ...*" Dropping to her knees by her bed, Brielle shut her eyes and nearly fell asleep as she uttered the French prayer she'd learned in childhood, "Forgive me whatsoever I have done amiss this day, and keep me all this night, while I am asleep. I desire to lie down under thy care, and to abide forever under thy blessing. Amen."

The linens she'd washed and dried felt smooth and clean against her skin, the open window admitting a refreshing night wind. Her last thought was of the scout, Ross, and if the troubling news he'd brought was true.

The Sabbath dawned bright.

Griffiths, however, was as dark as a thundercloud, his bellow rousing them from where he stood on the stair's landing below. "There'll be no rest for those who shirk their work! Up and in the fields, Titus. The Indian corn is in dire want of water."

Yanked awake, Brielle spilled from her bed, wondering how Titus fared in the night. He needed rest, his injuries salved again, but Griffiths had other plans. She cracked open her door to watch his small frame, head down, slowly descend the stairs as Griffiths ordered.

Their master hadn't lied. Across from the tavern the fields with their ridges and furrows were parched, the soil crusty and the plants limp. Titus would need to go to and from the spring, watering all the corn he could while wishing for rain. The wheat they could do little about. It would take an army of men to soak it, and they must pray and rely on the weather instead.

With no breakfast—for Griffiths withheld that, too—Titus limped to the corn field. Brielle dressed hurriedly, her hopes for the day dashed like dropped crockery. She was hard pressed to keep her frustration and fury in check as she went downstairs to breakfast, Tamsen following. A few lodgers were seated at trestle tables in the public room, Griffiths' enslaved serving them.

Entering the kitchen, Brielle had a dish of tea then slipped her uneaten toast into her pocket along with a boiled egg and greasy bacon. Once outside the tavern, she grabbed an empty bucket and gourd dipper, hastening to the spring that burbled in back of the milk house. Sunlight warmed her capped head and linen-clad shoulders as she filled the bucket and walked to the fields. Titus hadn't made much progress, sure to earn him more of Griffiths' ire.

Unaware of her approach, he finished a long, uneven row then swung round to return to the spring. Unclouded joy shone in his face at the sight of her. They were out of view of the tavern now at the back of the field. She passed him the breakfast she'd pocketed, her shadow shielding him from the sun as he wolfed it down.

She patted her other pocket. "I have salve too should you need it."

He looked up at her, eyes damp. "My legs are stinging like yellow jackets."

She took care of that, too, as he finished the toast and took a long drink of spring water. Thanking her, he returned to work, saying nothing when she began helping, dripping a gourd full of water on several plants at once as she went down her row. Only ankle-high, the corn made her wish it was full grown so they could hear its delightful rustle in the wind and seek its sweet shade. Sweat ran in rivulets from her hairline to her chin, dampening her shift and stays beneath her linen dress.

Titus removed his hat and fanned his shining face. "Hot as Hades."

Across the way, settlers began gathering at the front of the tavern. The preacher had just arrived on an old bay horse. Brielle felt a pang at his steadfastness. Many of these gospel men rarely reached the age of thirty, exposed to so many dangers. Knowing it made Brielle's own circumstances less loathsome. At least she had a place to lay her head and a meal day by day.

"Go on and hear the preaching," Titus urged, knowing how much Sabbath sermons meant to her.

Brielle continued her watering. "I'd rather be here."

His features tightened. "If Griffiths sees you helping me he might whip you, too."

She said nothing more, just resumed their shared task. It was still morning, more of the settlement gathering in fair weather. Some sat in the shade of the giant elms clustered around the tavern while others settled on the porch. Soon there'd be a lull for a meal then the sermon would resume till supper. The preacher's voice carried far though it didn't reach the field.

So far they'd watered only a quarter of the corn as the sun sizzled and insects swarmed. Thankfully the spring was west of the porch and they could travel back and forth between outbuildings without much notice. Where Griffiths was she didn't know. Usually he kept to his office adjoining the bar during the Sabbath.

Lightheaded, Brielle rued having only tea for breakfast. Titus seemed to sag, too, despite eating, his shoulders slumped, his skin crimson where the whip had cut him. She set her jaw and passed to the next row, batting her gourd dipper at a pesky fly. They continued on one hour. Two.

Toward noon the sharp crack of a rifle made them both turn toward the tavern. Across the wide, dusty road the familiar yard and porch swung violently from calm to chaos. Screams rent the air as more firing jarred harshly with eerie, undulating war cries. All the breath left Brielle as gathered settlers and tavern guests fell before a painted rush of warriors. The distressed whinny of stabled horses sounded before they were driven into the open, spared only to be stolen.

Titus took a step back, his voice a squeak. "Indians."

Grabbing his sleeve, Brielle yanked him to the hard, unforgiving ground. Her heart began an erratic gallop making her more breathless. They lay flat in the dirt, side by side, their heads barely raised enough to see over the leafing corn to the carnage. Bile burned the back of her throat as Griffiths rushed out of the tavern and fired his musket only to be tomahawked on the steps. Two Indians lay unmoving in the grass while another swarm of painted warriors cut down more settlers, many unarmed, before rushing into the tavern amid more screaming and shouting.

"Tamsen …" Titus choked on his sister's name.

Brielle searched for the girl but failed to see who lay upon the ground. Had she been indoors or out? Had she escaped? Thick woods behind the tavern made a fine hiding spot.

Lord, let her have gotten away.

Soon it was over save the sigh of the wind and the buzzing of insects in the field. Lying so long, Brielle felt melted upon the hot ground, unable to move or even speak. Titus's head was on his hands as if he couldn't bear to look any longer.

Could the Indians see them?

Warriors reappeared on the tavern porch, their tomahawks poking at this or that as they walked about. Next they raided outbuildings and took what they pleased, tying goods to the stolen horses, sacks of grain from the storehouse, even smokehouse meat. Then they gathered their dead, the feathers in their dark hair fluttering in a sudden gust of heated wind.

4

The deeper into Virginia he journeyed the more Bleu's hackles rose. Approaching the Great Road and Fort Loudoun at the northern entrance of the Shenandoah Valley, a passing scout confirmed sign of a war party. Upwards of twenty—and moving fast. Sometimes these warriors came to steal horses or cattle. Other times they ambushed travelers or far-flung homesteads, capturing women and children.

The scout rode on to spread a warning, toward LeHew and Helltown, places Bleu usually shunned given their rough reputation as a ferry crossing. He kept to streams and creeks and off the main trails to hide his own passing. The last time he'd crossed the Alleghenies he'd dispatched a Lenape intent on his scalp. Rarely did he strike but when it was kill or be killed he had no choice.

Wary, he rode on through woods so thickly leafed not even a sliver of light reached the forest floor. The everlasting gloom mirrored his mood. In contrast, his destination—the Rivanna River settlement—seemed *le paradis sur terre*. Heaven on earth. Settled. Serene. There, from his unfinished house in the foothills, these formidable mountains were a mere smudge of blue to the west.

This was what kept him going yet caused him to lose his way. Preoccupied with his rumbling stomach, he was remembering Sylvie's *cretons* and *fricot* and *gateau*. And the endearing way she always rushed to greet him, excited as a girl, the girl she'd been long ago in Acadie. Smiling and laughing, without a care. Those homecomings remained among his richest memories.

Dangerously distracted, he slowed his pace and reined in Windigo at the wood's edge. He'd nearly ridden into a wide, open clearing with fenced pasture and fields culminating in a crossroads, a three-story structure barely visible beyond a stand of sycamores and oaks.

Long minutes ticked past and no movement nor sound came from what appeared to be a tavern and outbuildings, just the timeless song of cicadas, the rhythmic rattle he'd been listening to all his life. He ran a linen sleeve across his damp brow as his alarm spiked. Something here was awry. The place bespoke danger ... destruction.

Death.

Brielle and Titus stayed in the cornfield, unmoving, for what seemed hours as the sun shifted and sank to the west. Finally, reaching out, she squeezed his nearest hand, blinking as black spots filled her vision.

Could one faint from sheer fear?

Their discarded buckets were near and so she managed to drag one toward them, bringing a gourd dipper to Titus's lips. He drank thirstily and then she did the same, the both of them emptying the bucket of tepid water meant for the corn.

"I've never been so affrighted," he whispered. "I don't want to move."

"Somebody will come by soon." Truly, folks were always coming and going. Eventually some passerby would help. The thought of returning to the tavern amid so much bloodshed made her dizzy all over again. "Perhaps we should wait till then."

"But what if my sister ain't dead and needs us?"

That possibility brought Brielle to her knees. Titus did the same, wincing slightly, the back of his welted legs sunburnt.

"What if the Indians come back?" Fear marred his features as he dropped back down to the dirt, raising puffs of dust. "Some of them raiders might still be waiting. Hiding."

Her gaze swept the frightful scene. Should they crawl to the edge of the field just in case?

"Stay here," she whispered. "Let me ..."

"What? Nay!" His voice became a strangled plea. "We have no weapon other than these blasted gourds."

Praying silently, Brielle took a deep breath and pushed past her terror. With another look at the tavern, she bent low and started toward it, a prayer on her lips. Every step cost her, her knees jelly. Wiping her damp palms on her apron, she stood upright and crossed the rutted crossroads worn down by countless horses and wagons.

Wind stirred the trees about the tavern, chilling her despite the day's heat. The sound of rustling leaves held the ominous music of an Indian rattle like the one Griffiths kept in his office alongside his collection of arrowheads. Her stomach cramped as she stood in the shade of the biggest oak and looked at the fallen. Flies were already hovering. Other preying creatures would soon follow. She feared panthers the most.

Her gaze swung wide, searching for any sign of life among the bloodied and battered.

Tamsen lay across the porch steps, her wounds too grave for her small frame. *Oh, Titus.* She clasped a hand to her mouth as horror clawed at her. Her concern made her careless for her own safety. But surely all the Indians were gone.

Choked, she turned back to the field to make sure Titus was still there. Still safe. Her senses were muddled—stubborn black spots still a–dance before her eyes—yet she distinctly heard a horse. Had help arrived? She swung unsteadily toward the sound and saw a lone rider coming from the west.

The stranger rode up in a storm of dust and dismounted a stone's throw away from her, his features hidden beneath the shade of his wide-brimmed hat. Something about him sent her back a step. His many weapons—the tomahawk hanging from his waist— seemed a warning. With a little cry, she stumbled backwards as her jellied knees gave way and the world went black.

Bleu dismounted, torn between what needed tending to first. The fainting woman—or the fallen. So many fallen. Here was evidence of the latest uprising. The war party had struck hard then moved on.

"Stop, mister!"

A shout behind him made him turn, his hand resting on the hilt of his belted knife. But it was only a small boy, the terror in his face vivid as war paint. He came between Bleu and the woman in the indigo dress, arms flung out as if he would protect her. Confusion filled his face as he looked at Bleu who stood stone still. Instinct told him the Indians had struck hours ago and this boy and woman had hidden somewhere, somehow.

Bleu kept his voice low. "I'm here to help, not hurt."

Tears shone in the boy's troubled eyes.

Bleu took a step toward the woman and the boy's hands dropped to his sides. On her back, her cap torn away by the wind, she lay facing away from him, eyes closed in a dead faint. "Let's get her out of the sun."

With a nod, the boy retrieved her cap then pointed as Bleu lifted her off the ground. "There's a spring behind the milk house—shade."

Bleu searched the shadows as he walked. The woman was small in stature and easily moved but he paid her scant attention, their safety foremost.

"She's more hungry than scared." The boy hovered, his alarm palpable. "She fainted 'cause she gave me her breakfast."

Kneeling, Bleu placed her in shaded grass, removed a handkerchief from his pocket, and wet it in the bubbling spring. Gently, he bathed her face, noting the fine features and pale-as-milk skin with the exception of her tanned, work-worn hands. Her braid trailed over her shoulder, a burnished amber-brown that reminded him of warm, sun-struck molasses. She was frightfully thin though there was no doubt she was a woman. A *belle femme*.

He looked at the boy, trying to lessen his terror by talking. "Is she often in the habit of giving you her meals?"

He nodded, slightly shamefaced as if caught in a trespass. "She's like that."

"What happened to your legs?"

"Griffiths whipped me for leaving the smokehouse door ajar."

"Griffiths?"

"Our bondsman." The boy looked toward the tavern, a strange mixture of relief and grief in his expression. "Well, he ain't no more."

Slowly, the woman sat up, her green eyes widening at the sound of approaching horses. An expletive split the silence as an armed party slowed near the front of the tavern. Bleu tucked the wet cloth into the woman's hand and stood.

"Militia," she said quietly. "Settlers from outlying farms."

He nodded, glad he wouldn't have to bury so many he didn't know. He extended a hand and helped her to her feet though she continued to regard him warily as if he was one of the war party.

"Wait here," he told her and the boy.

5

*B*rielle fastened her gaze on the stranger's stalwart, linen-clad shoulders as if he could keep her upright. For a few frantic seconds, scared witless, she'd feared this man was one of the warriors. Concerned someone might think him a party to the massacre had her hurrying after him as he joined the grim-faced men combing the tavern grounds.

Though she didn't know his name, his appearance proclaimed him of two nations. Métis? She'd seen Indian delegations pass by on their way to Williamsburg to meet with the governor but few half-bloods. This man was a striking blend of both worlds. Beaded buckskin and linen. Moccasins and felt hat. Midnight black hair. And his eyes—such a startling, striking blue that went straight to the heart, arrow sharp.

"Afternoon, Miss Farrow." The local militia captain touched the brim of his tricorn. "Glad you're still standing."

"Thank you, Captain Draper." She put an arm around Titus's shoulders and brought him nearer. "We were in the fields when they struck."

"A blessed escape, then." He looked to the militia who'd finished searching the tavern.

"There's seven inside," said one. "All dead and two scalped."

"I count twenty-two outside," another man said.

Brielle gestured to the stranger. "That man near the stables happened by first. I don't yet know his name."

"Galant." He approached, his gaze never settling. Did he think the Indians might return? "I found sign on the way here from Fort Pitt as did another scout. Likely a large war party—Shawnee and Delaware—moving fast."

"Just as I reckoned." Draper's brow tightened. "Anything else?"

"This has the mark of Bemino—Killbuck, some call him." Galant looked north. "Once he was friendly to the whites along the Wappocomo Valley, mainly the south fork of the Potomac, but has turned hostile since."

"Killbuck, aye. A French ally during the last war." Draper looked at him. "Where are you headed?"

"The Rivanna River. I usually travel north of here from Fort Pitt but once I picked up the war party's trail, I kept south but too late to raise an alarm and stop the bloodshed."

One man removed his hat. "Needs be we make a list of the dead though few of us are able."

"I can read and write." Brielle smoothed her rumpled apron with her hands. "I'll get a quill and ink and paper from Mr. Griffiths' office."

Draper held up a hand. "Tell us what happened first."

She took a breath, feeling like her knees might buckle again as she explained all that had transpired when she and Titus had been in the cornfield, from calm to chaos.

Would she ever be able to unsee the carnage?

"No captives taken?"

"They only took their dead. Four, to my reckoning. And several stolen horses."

They fell silent and she went for writing implements. Head down, stepping around the worst of it, she entered the tavern's front door. Returning with a lap desk, she sank down on the grass to record what needed recording as the men went round, identifying the dead. The scratching of her quill continued as the list grew, the ink splattered. Raising the hem of her apron, she swiped at her tears. When she'd finished, the men began talking amongst themselves.

Duties were assigned. Some would ride out and notify next of kin. Others had burial detail. If they tarried, scavengers would encroach. Captain Draper would inform the Frederick County seat and the authorities there once Brielle finished the list.

Not wanting to return inside after what she'd witnessed, she hesitated. Mr. Galant looked at her in question and held out a hand. She handed him the lap desk in answer as he sent Titus to the outbuildings in search of shovels.

Turning back to her, he said, "Go inside out of the sun and find something to eat. You need your strength."

She hesitated, afraid of what she'd find in the kitchen. As if sensing her struggle, he accompanied her to the back of the house. He went in first and then motioned her inside. The kitchen was blessedly empty. Cook had fallen in the hall.

Brielle's concern returned to Titus. "The boy, Titus Owens … his sister was cut down on the porch steps. Could you cover her with a sheet?" Hurrying to the nearest linen closet, she retrieved one. "She's red-haired. Young. You won't mistake her."

Stoic, he took the sheet and left the lap desk on the kitchen table before returning outside.

Lifting the lid of a pot in the ashes, she saw it held stew. A loaf of untouched bread sat on the open door of the bake oven. Butter and preserves and pickles waited on the table alongside a round of cheese. Oddly, the Indians had left the Sabbath meal untouched.

How was she to eat one bite?

At twilight, when all were buried in a common grave, the three of them sat at the kitchen table, Brielle and Titus across from the stranger. Bowing their heads, they each said silent grace. None of them had much appetite. They drank freely of the cider Griffiths had painstakingly made last autumn, its tang lingering on Brielle's tongue.

A few militia members remained to stand guard outside, the tavern's doors and windows shuttered and barred, the place barricaded as the dire news spread. Brielle wondered what would have happened to them had Mr. Galant not volunteered to stay.

Titus tore at a piece of bread, chewing in small bites. "When will you move on, mister?"

"Call me Bleu," he said with a wink. "I feel ancient when anyone calls me mister."

Bleu? Sylvie tried to keep her mind on her meal. *Bleu Galant.*

"I'll move on once I learn what's to happen here." By here he meant the two of them, surely, for his glance took in Brielle. He continued, thoughtful. "For now, tell me how it is you came to be at the tavern and how much time you have left as indentures."

Titus held his tongue and so she said, "I lack two years till my freedom dues."

"And you?" Bleu asked him, pouring them all more cider.

"Seven. My parents are dead, and I was bound out with my sister since no one else could take us."

Brielle listened, moved to tears again. No boy of eight should be bereft of everything, including the only family member he had left.

Bleu's attention returned to Brielle. "You're schooled."

She met his eyes, struck hard by their vibrant hue all over again. "I learned to read and write long ago at a city school founded by Friends—Quakers. Since coming here, I borrow books from Mr. Griffiths' library when he's away."

"The city?" He swallowed a spoonful of stew as if tempting them to do the same.

"Philadelphia." She paused, realizing she hadn't told him her name. "I'm Gabrielle Farrow."

"Ah ..." His eyes lit like candleflame. "Gabrielle ... *très française*."

"My father was English, my Mother French." She sensed his pleasure at the revelation. "I go by Brielle."

He continued eating without looking at her. "Do you speak *français*?"

The musicality of his words reached soul deep. Her mother's voice seemed to echo instead, bringing a sharp homesickness. For a moment she simply stared at him before she took up her own spoon. "Long ago I did. I've forgotten much of it. Few speak French here ..."

"She taught me a few words." Titus swallowed another small bite. "*Merci. Pardon. Bon.*"

A few, *oui*, if only to hold tight to her heritage. They continued to eat slowly in silence, more attuned to what was happening outside the kitchen.

Titus looked up from his half-finished meal as if eating somehow slighted his sister's memory. "What do you think'll happen to us now that the master's dead?"

Bleu took another drink. "Your former bondsman may have an heir who'll take his place or sell the tavern."

Titus's face fell. Brielle sensed his fear. The unknown was always frightening no matter how many times you faced it. Odd that this stranger had happened by when he did given he usually went further north, as he'd said. She cast about for some deeper meaning to their meeting and came up empty. He was simply another traveler, a frontiersman, who'd be on his way like so many who came to the tavern's crossroads from all directions.

"Did you help bury all them folks?" Titus held his spoon aloft. "My sister, too?"

"*Oui*, I did," Bleu said quietly. "In a clean linen sheet Miss Farrow gave me. A decent burial is *necessaire*, *non*?"

Brielle listened, torn between thankfulness and regret. Glad to be alive but still in servitude. Disbelieving despite death all around them. Would the shock of surviving simply because she'd followed Titus into the cornfield ever fade?

Might God have something more in mind for her?

Titus sighed. "I'm sorry for my sister but I know she's safe in heaven."

"Safe," Brielle echoed, believing it with all her heart. "And happy and whole."

"And we're still together here." His worried eyes met hers and she tried to smile in reassurance.

They were still together, for the time being, come what may.

6

How odd it felt to return to her attic room in a tavern emptied of guests but guarded by a few of the militia. But in truth, Brielle would have felt safe with only Bleu Galant defending them. His presence and weapons held her in a sort of horrified awe, the colorful beading on his tomahawk suggesting an equally colorful story untold. He likely slept with all the accoutrements of war on his cot downstairs in the tavern passageway. Such was the way of woodsmen.

It hadn't taken her long to realize he was as decisive, quick-witted, and observant as he was powerfully made. He could have reopened the tavern and run it himself had he wanted. The chilling scar that flanked his left brow to his jawline failed to mar his appeal. He was by far the most arresting man she'd ever seen—and she'd seen plenty in the city and at the crossroads.

In his presence she felt small. Nothing but a bondservant with little to recommend her. Yet she was full of big questions. Where had he come from? Where was he going? Did he have a home? Suddenly every facet of him intrigued her. He glittered like a rough-cut gem beyond her reach.

Now, hours after meeting him, she lay atop her bed, ears tuned to the slightest threatening sound beyond the open window as he played across her conscience.

Bleu.

It suited him, strong yet comely, much like the French words and phrases threading his speech. *That* she hadn't expected. Hearing her mother's native tongue again cracked open a bitter-sweet door to the past she'd tried to keep shut. It hurt too much to remember. Yet his use of it won her over just the same.

When she awoke the next morning to the rooster crowing, she dressed hurriedly with a strange anticipation despite all the work awaiting her. She heard Titus on the other side of the wall, in the room he'd shared with his sister. The soreness she felt over Tamsen now set in as the shock of her death wore off. To think of all those buried overwhelmed her. Too much for one soul to hold.

She crept downstairs, unsure of what she'd find, smelling coffee and bacon wafting from the kitchen. Warily, she darted a glance at Griffiths' ransacked office. A mail bag lay on the floor, the latest sack sent to the tavern for those in the settlement. Because she was learned, Griffiths had her handle the post, passing out letters and recording who came to pick them up or sent them, always collecting the required pence. Of all her tasks, this was her favorite for it allowed her a little dreaming. The novelty of the mail broke the monotony of her days.

Boston. New York. Savannah. Williamsburg. York Town.

Places she'd only heard of but never been. Two more years and she could go anywhere she pleased once she'd collected her freedom dues. Though she might never be a lady of leisure surely there was a chance for rest, kinder work, the ability to enjoy life's little pleasures aside from the Sabbath. Yet that was a frightening prospect too.

How did one go anywhere when one had no ties to anyone?

The passageway was empty of its splintered furniture, even the cot Bleu Galant had slept on. She followed the aroma coming from the kitchen, stopping in the open doorway. Their guest—if one could call him that—was making breakfast. Turning bacon in a skillet while something equally delicious emanated from the bake oven.

For a moment she stood openmouthed before her gaze swiveled from him to the set table. Rather than being served, he was serving them? To her utter astonishment he'd placed flowers from the tavern's garden in a small pitcher at the table's center. Pale pink roses and purple irises and butter-yellow day lilies. Somehow it seemed he'd picked them for her. Or was she so starved for attention and affection it made her more fanciful?

Without turning around he said, "Good morning, *Mademoiselle* Farrow."

Did he have eyes in the back of his head?

"Good morning, *Monsieur* Galant."

"Bleu," he countered, looking over his shoulder with a half-smile.

Flustered, she sat down at the table, biting her lip lest she offer to help. What could she possibly do given he had all in hand?

"May I call you Brielle?"

His pronunciation was perfect. So very French. If he'd not won her over already the way he said her name would have settled it. "*Oui* … Bleu."

He poured a cup of coffee and handed it to her. Had he milked the cow, too? She saw no cream yet the cow wasn't bawling. At once he brought cream in a small pitcher. Amused, she wondered. Would he churn the butter or leave that for her to do? Though he was reassuringly near, she still feared going beyond the back door …

"I took liberties and turned the cow out to pasture and gathered eggs." He gestured to his weapon leaning against the wall. "Safely."

She tried to imagine him picking flowers and doing chores encumbered with a gun as he turned back to the hearth and reached for a spatula, flipping ... *plogues?*

Again she felt that bittersweet, disbelieving tug. *Plogues* had often graced her family's table—steaming, buttery stacks over-flowing with molasses.

"We have no *cretons*," he lamented, placing a stack of steaming *plogues* near her. "But one miracle at a time ..."

She smiled. "I imagine you make excellent *cretons*, too."

"On occasion." He looked back at her, eyes alight. "When you live alone for so long, you learn to do all manner of things."

Surprise pinched her. Had he no wife? No sweetheart? How was that even possible? He was so *beau* he took her breath away.

Her musings ended when Titus appeared. Despite his red-dened eyes—from crying or a sleepless night?—he looked more pleased than surprised. Rarely did they sit down for a breakfast feast together. That was reserved for tavern guests.

"Thank'ee." Titus surveyed the spread in wonder and took one of the *plogues* in question.

"I've eaten these since I was a boy like you in Acadie," Bleu told him, setting molasses on the table. "A sort of pancake."

He looked at Bleu with bleary eyes. "Is it wrong to be hungry when my sister's just been buried?"

"*Non*, it simply means you are still alive."

They bowed their heads and said their own silent grace. The scent of the flowers, the pop of the hearth, the delicious break-fast she didn't have to make rendered Brielle speechless. Such a comfortable, companionable quiet so unlike the stilted, cower-ing silence when Griffiths was near. Her relief that he was gone shamed her as much as it assuaged her. Already the tavern's tense mood had been broken.

"Since we cannot all safely venture outside at the moment, we can tend to matters inside." Bleu's gaze swept the kitchen. "I will straighten your master's office, to start, if you can find other useful work to do."

Brielle nodded. "I'll ready the bedchambers for the next lodgers once I clean the kitchen."

"I can tidy the bar," Titus said, already retrieving a broom.

Bleu rose from the table while Brielle began gathering the empty dishes. "I heard the tavern's owner—Griffiths—has an heir."

Oh? She knew of no heir. Would he be like Griffiths? Cold, shrewd, avaricious?

She watched Bleu leave the kitchen, wishing he was the rightful owner and there'd be no end to this current arrangement. Already she felt bereft at the thought of his leaving. He'd been uncommonly kind to them. He'd stayed on to be their defender, delaying his own travels, when most men would have been on their way, leaving them to the militia in the meantime.

Why had he lingered?

7

*B*leu picked up the broken furniture, thrown about and tomahawked beyond repair, and fed it to the hearth's fire he'd made. Light streamed across Griffiths' desk that he guessed was untidy at the best of times. Littered with papers and spilled ink and pounce, some of the damaged ledgers were beyond recovery.

Where had Griffith kept the paperwork for his indentures? Usually a contract was torn in two so that each party, master and servant, could have a portion. Once the contract was fulfilled, the two pieces were brought together to prove the authenticity of the papers. He eyed a corner safe, locked, and wondered its contents.

Working through the forenoon, he saved what he could, setting aside what might be restored, and cleaned up the rest. He longed to be outside on so fair a day. By now, had he not been waylaid, he'd have been far closer to the Rivanna River. Yet whatever kept him here gave him a measure of peace despite the tragedy. It would be wrong to ride on in the face of so much ruination—and he felt obliged to see that the woman and boy changed hands safely.

Brielle Farrow. Titus Owens.

He could hear them both elsewhere in the tavern. Titus continued to straighten the bar's disorder while the soft patter of

Brielle's footsteps sounded overhead as she came in and out of rooms and opened and closed doors.

Finished with Griffiths' office, he began a slow walk about the tavern's interior, peering out window after window on all floors, climbing to the attic eaves where Titus told him they slept. Here the territorial view was expansive, reaching to the Blue Mountains and beyond. Coming downstairs again, he stepped onto the porch to find Brielle already there talking to one of the militia.

She turned toward him. "Titus asked me if you could take us to the gravesite."

Her face was so entreating he'd have taken her to Philadelphia and back. "*Bien sûr.*"

Of course. "The chosen ground is well to the west of the tavern beyond the orchard."

"A comely place."

Titus appeared and Brielle took his hand, knowing this would be hard for him. "Perhaps you can make a grave marker for Tamsen. You're good at working with your hands, with wood."

"I reckon Griffiths won't begrudge me using his carving tools."

All those tools, of no use to their bondsman now.

"You could make a cross," she encouraged. "Tamsen would have liked that."

The day wore on, Titus helping Bleu with all the outside chores usually managed by eight tavern servants while Brielle kept busy inside. So far no new lodgers had appeared. Were they now wary of the crossroads? She didn't blame them. After so much carnage it might take time to return to its usual bustling routine.

Toward suppertime, Titus brought the woodworking tools inside. Head bent, he worked quietly in a corner while she prepared supper, wondering how long the militia would stay. They'd been eating in the public room. As it was, between kitchen and larder and despite the raiders pilfering supplies, she had enough to feed a small army. In a bold, unarmed moment, she'd even sneaked to the garden for more peas and new potatoes.

When Bleu returned inside at dusk, he plunged his head then his hands into a wash bucket near the back door. Watching him, she tried to keep from smiling as he stood upright, running his hands through his dark hair to slick it back, his queue ribbon falling to his booted feet.

"Permit me." Coming up behind him as he dried his hands on a clean linen towel, she retrieved it, standing on tiptoe to tie it into place. He held still as she made short work of the ribbon, securing it, her fingertips brushing the silk of his hair and finding it as soft as her own.

"*Merci.*" Turning round, he looked to the set table in question.

"Are you hungry?" she asked, retying her apron.

"Ravenous," he replied.

"I've made *cretons.*"

His eyes lit again, their deep blue startling her all over again. "*Merci.*"

A shyness beset her. "I might not have remembered my mother's recipe well though I often helped her cook ..."

He brought a finger to his lips briefly and she smiled as his hand fell away and he took a seat at the table, clearly ready to eat though she was still waiting on the bread.

"It's the least I can do after what you've done for us." She kept busy at the hearth with the meal's final touches as she talked. "Staying on here. Seeing to our wellbeing."

"I am in no hurry to get to where I am going. Not when a need arises."

Titus looked up from where he was whittling, wood shavings at his feet. "Where are you headed exactly?"

"To see my sister along the Rivanna River. She lives there with her husband and their six *enfants turbulents*."

Brielle nearly laughed at his phrasing. Six children, turbulent or not, seemed like heaven on earth.

Titus perked up. "What are their names?"

Bleu heaved a rare sigh as if he couldn't remember then recited with admirable ease, "Amélie, Jolie Corbin, Madeleine, Talbot, and Morgan Blackburn. There might be another by now. I haven't seen them for some time."

"And you're Uncle Bleu. I had an uncle once but he died in the war with my father," Titus murmured, returning to his whittling.

Brielle pulled a pan of pepper cake from the bake oven and fetched cider from the cellar before finally sitting down with them. Bleu said grace in French, his head bent and his hands fisted, elbows on the table. The rusty words seemed to unlock another door deep within, his honeyed speech playing in her mind like a melody.

"How many languages do you speak?" she asked, pouring him cider.

"Several Indian tongues though I prefer French and Mi'kmaq."

"Mi'kmaq?" Titus asked between bites.

"A tribe in Canada. My mother was Mi'kmaq and died when I was very young."

"Like mine," Titus murmured, buttering his bread.

Bleu studied the boy, sadness in his eyes. When he reached for the potted pork—the *cretons*—Brielle held her breath.

Taking up his knife, he spread it on leftover plogues from breakfast and took a bite. She felt she might burst when he swallowed and said, "Cinnamon, cloves, ginger, pepper ... *la perfection*."

Titus sampled it next, declaring it tasty, indeed, and she smiled her thanks. The scraping of empty plates as dishes emptied brought a sort of fulfillment she'd not felt for ... years. Once all the pewter and treenware were cleared away and washed, she took out her knitting while Titus continued his woodwork and Bleu returned with a book from Griffiths' office library. He disappeared again and hefted twin Windsor chairs. Positioning them by a window, he invited her to sit.

She lowered herself to the forbidden seat, feeling like a queen at court. All the while her head whirled along with her deeply smitten heart.

This cannot last. Take heed lest ye fall. Here is the love that came without warning.

Her knitting needles seemed clumsy in her hands, the yarn uncooperative. She kept her eyes on her lap as he opened his book, wanting to ask what he was reading. Rare it was to find a literate man. She had a sudden, whimsical wish he'd read aloud to her like her father had her mother. The beloved if hazy memory tightened her throat.

The night deepened and she lit candles, not the smelly tallow ones that curled her nose but the forbidden beeswax, their perfume spreading to the kitchen's corners. Griffiths was not here to stop her. She settled in, imagining them a family. She'd nearly forgotten what that was like. She'd never felt safer or more secure.

She wanted this night to have no end.

8

*A*fter a week, a party of men appeared. Bleu met them on the porch as the leader on a big bay horse dismounted. He approached, his gaze swinging wide as he surveyed the tavern like he owned it. Small, slim, and smug, he made up for it in arrogance.

"I'm the new proprietor of the *Rose and Crown* though I'm tempted to rename it the *Crimson Crossroads.*"

The men with him laughed but Bleu found no humor in it. Any goodwill he'd come onto the porch with vanished at the man's next utterance.

"And who are you?" His close-set eyes held disdain. "A hired hand?"

"My name's Galant." Bleu's hand rested on the leather pistol holster at his waist as Brielle and Titus appeared on the porch behind him. "And you are?" he continued, meeting the man's flighty gaze.

"Wade Griffiths, nephew and heir of the former owner." He looked at Titus then Brielle. "Are these my indentures? I was told some survived."

The gaze the man fastened on Brielle made Bleu want to draw his pistol. "These two were bound to your uncle. The rest are buried."

"A pity. I'll need more help then." He stepped onto the porch and ran a gloved hand down the scarred railing. "I suppose you're a temporary lodger. When will you be on your way?"

"When I'm sure Miss Farrow and the boy are in good hands."

Griffiths frowned. "I'll take possession immediately. My baggage wagon will arrive shortly. These heavily armed men you see with me are hired guards."

Hired ruffians, rather, who'd signed on immediately at the mention of a tippling-house. Bleu was far less inclined to leave now that he'd met them.

"You there—Miss Farrow—show me about the tavern while the boy sees to our horses." Griffiths pulled off his leather gloves. "But first a drink. We're all in need of rum or ale. I trust there's an abundance of both."

With that, Griffiths walked around Bleu and entered the tavern.

Brielle followed the younger Griffiths inside, dread descending like a black cloud. The older Griffiths was an unpleasant man but instinct told her his heir was worse. To her surprise, Bleu went into the bar and began serving the men drinks while Titus saw to their horses.

Once he'd whet his thirst he sought her out again while his companions kept to the bar, Bleu still behind the counter. Brielle waited in the passageway, determined to keep her distance from the man who'd demanded she show him his new holdings.

"The *Rose and Crown* is usually full," she began, gesturing to the large public room with its long tables and benches. Titus had done an admirable job of setting it to rights. "Being at a crossroads, folks come from all directions though we've had no one stay since that dire Sunday."

"Bad for business. I'll need to see accounts. Peruse ledgers." He frowned. "I trust the entire endeavor is profitable year round. I won't be privy to anything ill-managed."

"Your uncle kept his business accounts in his office." She crossed the passageway, glad Bleu had returned the Windsor chairs. "This room was ransacked but has since been righted."

He walked about, examining the less than full bookshelves flanking the hearth and a cracked window she'd not noticed before. Sitting down at the desk, he reached for a ledger then tossed it aside. "Carry on."

She'd never felt more like a servant. Dissatisfaction stiffened his features and left her wondering how he'd manage guests being so rude. He bristled with bad manners as did his hired hands in the bar. One had even spat tobacco onto the porch. Even now their raucous talk and laughter grated as Brielle led the way to the kitchen.

"Quite commodious," he said as he poked his head into the larder then lifted the lid on a pot of stewed chicken and dumplings she'd made. "Can you cook?"

"I can though my duties till now were mostly serving meals and readying rooms. The former cook lies buried in back of the orchard with others killed that day."

His unnerving gaze pinned her again. "How did you survive?"

She avoided his eyes, reaching for a spoon to stir the bubbling pot. "I was working in the cornfield with Titus Owens."

"Fortunate. You seem competent enough though that remains to be seen. Owens is a bit young. I need able men, not boys."

Her thoughts swung to Bleu. Might he stay on a bit longer? She sensed a man of Bleu's mettle couldn't abide such bad company. For a trice she rued the passing of the elder Griffiths, sensing the worst sort of servitude stretched ahead of her.

Upstairs they went from room to room as she weathered his criticisms of what she had no control over. The linens, though clean, bore stains. Threadbare rugs needed replacing. Chipped furniture required mending. At least he couldn't complain about dust and cobwebs for she'd seen to that.

She wouldn't show him the back stairs secreted behind a door that led to their servant's quarters and wound down to the kitchen. That seemed too intimate, a trespass of her hard-won privacy. He'd undoubtedly discover it in time but not on her watch. The thought made her shiver. For now he seemed intent on returning to the bar.

Once the crossroads and tavern resumed its bustle, he'd be too busy to pay her attention or so she hoped. Fear could only hold the backcountry captive for so long. Until the next attack, if there was one, crops and livestock needed tending, travelers and lodgers, too.

Her relief was short lived. The very idea of Bleu Galant riding away sank her spirits. Their time together had been as memorable as it had been short. His freedoms were not lost on her. His ability to go wherever and whenever he pleased seemed a heaven-sent privilege.

"Why so downcast, Miss Farrow?" Griffiths' probing question was more accusation.

She started down the steps, unable to speak past the knot in her throat.

"Answer me." On the landing he reached for her, his fingers curling around her forearm like talons. "As your new master I'll not abide any insolence. You'll mind your temper and your tongue."

Pulling her arm free, she continued down the stairs. "If I'm downcast it's because of a brutal raid and the tavern changing hands. There's little room for mirth."

He said nothing more but she sensed his ire. To her relief, he returned to the bar. Bleu was still serving—or was he overseeing? The front door was open wide and she stood in the doorframe, breathing in the fresh late spring air and hoping Titus would return from the stables. She still felt wary of being outside since the militia had dispersed with the heir's arrival.

Now with Wade Griffiths here, the enemy was within.

9

By suppertime, Griffiths and his men were confoundedly drunk, playing cards and smoking and gambling, seemingly caring little about what went on elsewhere in the empty tavern.

"'Tis a blessing in disguise," Brielle said quietly as she followed Bleu upstairs.

He'd removed an iron bolt from a second-story shutter, thinking it wouldn't be missed. She marveled that she hadn't had to broach her need for safety, nor had Bleu elaborated. He'd simply told her he was going to safeguard her room. Gratitude filled her as she watched him work.

"Have you seen this man before?" he asked her.

"Nay. Mr. Griffiths never mentioned any family, nor an heir."

"Never?" Bleu finished securing the bolt and met her eyes. "At least that you know of?"

She shook her head, combing through the few conversations with the master she'd been privy to or had overheard. "He was a hard man, little given to conversation, even with guests."

"He never mistreated or abused you?"

Heat prickled her neck and she looked to her scuffed shoes. "He whipped me once when I first came here but after that he left me alone."

"He overworked you."

She opened her hands in answer, her palms covered in calluses. Her mother's hands had been pale and soft. Genteel hands. Her father's, given his trade, had been rougher than her own. "Griffiths had a hard time keeping help. Even his enslaved and indentured ran away."

"I'm unfamiliar with contracts such as yours other than that they vary from place to place." He pocketed the borrowed turn screw. "Do you know your rights?"

"Per my contract, I pledged my obedience and cannot divulge my master's secrets. Legally, I can be sold or loaned to someone else without my permission. I cannot wed without the master's consent nor can I spend any money."

"So, your life is not your own until you gain your freedom." He went to the window and looked out, and she wondered what he thought of her treasured view. "I'm now a paying guest. I'll not leave till lodgers fill the rooms again. Then you'll have a measure of safety if not peace."

Safety if not peace.

Sometimes he expressed what she thought or felt as if privy to her every turn of mind and emotion, her every mood. Did he sense her high regard of him, too?

Thanking him, she started down the steps, wondering what would happen next. For now, she sought the refuge of the kitchen and the meal she'd prepared with him in mind. Last night shone in her memory like a star, the three of them in this room, the outside world held at bay. Peace had blanketed her for a few hallowed hours. Even the tragedy had been pushed to the furthest reaches of her mind as she knitted and Bleu had read and Titus had finished fashioning the cross to mark Tamsen's grave.

"Are you hungry?" she asked Titus when he appeared.

He nodded, looking sad. He was not only missing his sister, he was as unsettled as she about their new master. She read his thoughts like Bleu read hers. The only difference was that she'd known Titus for a few years, not a few days.

"Griffiths came in and raided the larder," he whispered. "Said he prefers to eat in the bar."

"Oh?" She sat down opposite him. They used to serve the former Griffiths in his office. "Everything's a bit topsy-turvy now."

She'd noticed Griffiths seemed to tread lightly with Bleu near, even avoiding them. He'd only barked at her once in private. Bleu seemed more in charge than their new master which left her both amused and muddled.

Titus's small hand crept across the table to where hers rested, reaching around the slightly wilted flowers in their pitcher. "I'm glad you're safe." He squeezed her fingers. "I wouldn't want to be here with you gone."

Her throat knotted again as Bleu came in. Without a word, he began to dish up their supper, serving them when she'd meant to serve him. Titus let go of her hand as they bowed their heads and said grace, the words drowned out by loud laughter down the passageway.

Tonight's meal was anything but peaceful. The sudden arrival of guests took Griffiths away from his card game as they sought lodging. Titus left his unfinished supper to see to their horses while Brielle was summoned to show them their rooms. When they told her they didn't need a meal, she returned to the kitchen and found Bleu gone, the back door open.

She went outside, breathing deeply of the warm twilight air, and saw him coming from the stables, a pipe in hand. She'd all but forgotten to put the tavern's used pipes in their iron cradles.

She'd need to clean them in the bake oven for their next paying guests.

Would Wade Griffiths upbraid her about that?

Bleu saw Brielle moving about the garden with a basket on one arm, her petticoats swaying in the warm night wind. Her humble linen garments were scrupulously clean tip to toe, from her apron and cap to her stockings, her worn shoes polished. She reminded him of his fastidious sister but the comparison ended there.

Though her dress was faded and mended there was no doubt Gabrielle Farrow was *enchanteresse*. He continued to search—and half-wish—for some flaw and found none. If she was this *ravissante* in plain clothes what would she look like in fancy dress? Her only blemish was her alarming leanness and her callused hands.

He'd seen women who were as hard as they were beautiful. Brielle's beauty went deeper. Despite her hardships, she maintained a sweetness of spirit, an earnestness that put him at ease, a humility and kindness that drew attention to others and not herself. She had an extraordinary grace that belied her station. It left him flummoxed and fascinated.

He sat on a bench at the back of the garden, unable to look away from her though she wasn't looking at him. When he left, would the lovely imprint of her be engraved in his head if not his heart?

She soon had a basketful of blooms, again reminding him of Sylvie and the walled garden behind Orchard Rest. Here the carefully tended vegetables and flowers bespoke Brielle's tending. Someone had taken care to fence it in, safe from deer and rabbits and other ravagers.

Seeing him, she drew near, curiosity in her green gaze. "Your tobacco is fragrant though it isn't Tidewater nor Orinoco."

"*Tabac.*" He expelled a breath. "An Indian variety."

"Nor is your pipe Virginia clay."

"Soapstone." He held it aloft, the bowl glowing. "A gift from a Mohawk ally."

"'Tis ... *belle.*"

He studied her through the smoke's haze. "Is it my imagination or is your *français* coming back to you?"

"*Oui.*" She smiled and looked to her basket, her lashes like black fringe above the spots of color in her cheeks. "Only it is not quite like your Acadian French."

"Yours is more Québec French," he told her, remembering his time there. "Purer. More proper, perhaps."

She smiled at him and it seemed the sun was rising rather than setting. Beguiled he was, dangerously so. She was so close he wanted to reach out and take her hand and draw her onto the bench beside him. Fireflies drifted about them, tiny suspended lanterns in the twilight. He looked toward the stables. Titus's small outline appeared at the entrance then vanished as raised voices and laughter erupted from the bar.

Her face darkened. "I wish that you were my bondsman."

Quoi? He almost choked on his pipe smoke.

He met her eyes and a sort of lightning flashed between them. She was frightened. He could feel it. She dreaded his leaving. He knew that, too. But he was not her bondsman. He'd never own another soul, even an indenture, as long as he lived.

He couldn't even gather the words to reply nor did she seem to expect any. She simply turned and walked back to the tavern, more shadow than substance, a telling emptiness in her wake.

10

As the tavern filled again, Bleu lined his saddlebags with what was needed for continuing his journey. When Brielle appeared with a small jar of *cretons*, he tried to smile. Titus brought him his horse as he'd requested, knowing a farewell was imminent.

"I never asked your horse's name," the boy said, running a hand down the stallion's muzzle.

"Windigo," Bleu told him, tightening the saddle's girth. "It means *powerful monster* in Mi'kmaq."

"Your people in Canada?"

Bleu nodded. "You have a good memory. Brielle should teach you to read and write."

"She said the same but there's little time for learning."

"Make time for it." He swung himself up in the saddle, fighting the urge to take them in his arms as he did Sylvie and the children whenever he said farewell.

Brielle stood, hands clasped behind her back, looking wilted as a flower. Even Titus seemed crestfallen, face ruddy as if trying to hold his feelings in check. In the emotion of the moment none of them spoke. There was no word in Mi'kmaq for goodbye. Nor did Brielle say *adieu* or *au revoir*. The latter, in French, meant goodbye forever. He'd had many of those in his tumultuous, roving life. Only this time he couldn't abide it.

With a word to Windigo, Bleu turned away, prodding his horse forward. It took an iron will to keep from looking back.

Brielle wanted to say farewell and express her thanks, but the words hung in her throat and she felt choked. She simply stood there like a simpleton, buffeted by a wave of emotion strong enough to send her to her knees. All the security and peace she'd felt in Bleu's presence—to say nothing of her heart—seemed to have been wrapped up and stored in his saddlebags, leaving with him.

He rode away at a canter, his horse a fine mount for so fine a man. She imagined herself riding alongside him on a roan like the one she'd come on to the inn. It had been years since then. Horses were for people of means. Free people.

Waving his small, cocked hat for as long as he could, Titus returned it to his head and slipped his hand into hers. "Think we'll ever see him again?"

She could only squeeze his fingers in wordless anguish.

Her thoughts were swirling along with her emotions as Bleu Galant disappeared from sight and it seemed she'd only dreamed him up. But the hole he'd left was so blisteringly wide she felt burned. In him she'd glimpsed another sort of life, a blessed existence beyond her reach. He was headed toward that now, leaving her behind.

Letting go of Titus's hand, she headed back to the tavern as more travelers rode in, leaving their horses to him. She'd spied Griffiths on the porch as Bleu was leaving. He was often there, idle, talking with this one or that, rarely inclined to work, even in his uncle's office. As she started up the steps, he blocked her way.

His cold question held a sneer. "What is your tie to that man, Galant?"

"I have no tie." She passed by without looking at him. "None at all."

Truly, she'd not even felt at liberty to ask Bleu if he'd come round again. The backcountry was vast. This was not his usual route to travel. His destination was far beyond their crossroads, deeper into Virginia.

Heartsick, she returned to the kitchen, weaving through a throng of people in the passageway, mostly men interested in the bar rather than the public room. Faced with the multitude of tasks before her, she resumed breadmaking, the back door open to relieve the day's heat. The midday meal was almost upon them. Since she would act as cook until another was hired, Titus took her place as server in the public room.

The exchange wasn't without mishaps, earning Griffiths' ire. Already she'd burned bread and served rancid cider while Titus dropped crockery, including a Delft tobacco jar. He'd even spilled gravy in a man's lap. Since Griffiths showed no signs of hiring more help, she prepared for a long, grueling season when the tavern was busiest. But she would keep Titus's spirits up if she could. He was the sweetness in her world, her one tender tie.

That night she climbed the stairs to her attic refuge while the bar continued merry below. Lodgers came up and down the stairs, seeking their rooms or another drink or just the cooler air of the porch. Pressing a hand to her pinched back, she wished for a bath. Grease clung to her, her apron and petticoats stained and spotted beyond repair. At least Bleu hadn't seen her like this. She had no one to be presentable for once he'd ridden away, no reason to take pains with her appearance, and no time for it.

She could hear Titus toss fitfully on his bed as hot air pressed down on them beneath the eaves despite their open windows.

Tonight the top floor was an oven, and the dog days of July and August had yet to come.

Still, I will be thankful.

She was whole-bodied and well. She loved the child in the next room with all her heart. They had both escaped death that dreadful Sabbath day. For now, that was enough. Someday she would be free of this, free of Griffiths' leering looks, the endless, relentless drudgery of tavern life, the ongoing fear of punishment.

She sat near an open window, hoping for the slightest breeze. Weary as she was, her thoughts still swung to Bleu. Was he safe? How far down the valley was he? Did his heart leap at the thought of seeing his sister and her family again?

Lying down atop the cornhusk mattress, she dozed then jerked awake at a troubling sound. Had the door rattled or had it been a bad dream? Sensing a presence on the other side, she sat upright. The door rattled again. Someone waited, trying to gain entry. No lodger had ever disturbed her before. Most didn't know about the hidden back stair.

But now Wade Griffiths did.

If not for Bleu and the bolt, he could have simply pushed the door open. She started to shake, the night more frightful than it had ever been before. She was nearly as afraid as she'd been in the cornfield that day.

Yet spared by Bleu. And a blessed bolt.

11

leu crossed Opequon Creek and took a little-traveled
deer trail to reach Winchester, the county seat. On a rise
north of the settlement sat Fort Loudoun with its barracks, store-
houses, and well. *This vile post,* Colonel Washington had called the
square garrison with its diamond-shaped bastions and twenty-four
cannon built a few years before.

Once the site of a former Shawnee village, the settlement
now held a courthouse, an Anglican church, a jail, and a great
many poorly built houses. He rode down a main thoroughfare,
looking for lodging. Within a half hour he'd secured a room at
the *Golden Buck Inn,* a handsome two-story stone building on
Cameron Street that reminded him of the *Rose and Crown.* With
Windigo stabled, he was free to seek the courthouse.

As he walked toward the unfamiliar building, he weighed
what he was about to do. Since leaving the crossroads he'd not had
a moment's peace. Brielle's stoicism at his leaving hadn't fooled
him though she'd tried to put up a brave front. Titus's outright
dismay hadn't left his mind either

How was it possible to become so attached to two strangers in
so short a time? One in particular? He, a soul who roamed far and
wide, rootless and homeless, caught between two worlds in a sort

of no-man's-land, had experienced something he had no words
for in any language.

Seemingly overnight the *Rose and Crown* had become less than
respectable. A brawl broke out in the tavern yard over an accusation that someone had cheated at cards. Pewter candlesticks from
the public room and a ham from the smokehouse were filched.
Griffiths' mood became fouler and Brielle and Titus more chary.

A blur of heated days passed. And then at midnight, once again,
they climbed the stairs to the attic though the bar below refused to
quiet, surely disrupting lodgers' sleep. Never had she wanted the
older Mr. Griffiths back more than now. At least he maintained
order. Never had he tried to enter her room be it daylight or dark.
Once a sort of refuge and reprieve, nighttime held a new danger.

Bidding Titus goodnight, she slipped inside the dark, humid
space. When she raised her hand to draw the bolt her fingers met
rough wood instead. The sudden plummeting in her stomach
made her nauseous. Her safety—her slim security—vanished. In
the pale moonlight through the window she saw that the bolt
Bleu had put in place was missing. Never had she dreamt that possibility. It turned her to ice despite the stifling attic.

She wasted no time, crossing over to knock softly at Titus's
door. "Needs be I sleep in here tonight."

Yawning, he nodded and pulled out his trundle bed as she entered.
"You sleep on the topmost mattress and I'll lie nearer the floor."

But would this deter Griffiths? Titus's door had no lock, no
bolt ...

In minutes he was asleep, his steady half-snore like the rasp of
a saw. Eyes wide open, she listened for a footfall, a creak on the
stairs. Tomorrow she would rise even earlier, emptying chamber

pots and scrubbing floors and washing linens. She needed rest to face whatever needed facing, yet fear kept her from it.

An hour passed. She could tell by the slant of the moon. The slightest noise sent her heart racing. The footfall she dreaded was heard around three o'clock. A slow, shuffling step that bespoke an abundance of ale and ill intent. She heard the familiar groan of her door as it pushed open.

Breathless, her pulse ticking so hard it hummed in her ears, she summoned the only defense she had. Into the darkness of Titus's unlocked room she whispered the words she'd stitched onto a sampler she'd worked by her mother's side long ago.

I will both lay me down in peace, and sleep; For thou, Lord, only makest me dwell in safety.

Brielle pulled bread from the bake oven and sensed someone behind her. Setting the loaf on the trestle table, she met Griffiths' irate gaze. His bloodshot eyes were mere slits, his clothing disheveled. Reaching into his pocket he withdrew the iron bolt and tossed it onto the table with a little clatter.

"Don't lock me out, Miss Farrow."

Fury blotched his face scarlet. She took a step back, glad the table was between them or he might have struck her. Suddenly tongue-tied, she swallowed nervously. Perhaps silence was the best answer.

"Where were you last night?"

She didn't look at him. Taking up a knife, she began slicing roasted meat she'd pulled from the spit. "I slept elsewhere for my own wellbeing."

"Your *wellbeing*?" He snorted. "If you do it again I'll take you to court and charge you with running away. You'll be whipped and branded on the cheek with the letter *R*. I'll double your indenture time—or worse. No official in Virginia will believe the word of a bondswoman over her master."

True enough. She'd read advertisements for runaways in the *Virginia Gazette*. Even if they fled cruel conditions, they were often caught and their master's won. No matter that the charge was often a lie.

He reached out and took a piece of meat, downing it like a dog in two gulps. "No bolt nor lock. No sleeping elsewhere. Remember it or else."

When he left the kitchen her unsteady legs gave way. She sat down hard on the table's bench, staring at the bolt. Titus found her there, his expression alarmed as she was rarely idle.

"You all right?" he whispered. "Did Griffiths hurt you?"

"Nay." *Not yet.*

Clearly addled, Titus reached for a broom and started sweeping. "I snuck out to see Tamsen's grave and made sure my cross is still standing."

She looked at him, still disbelieving his sister lay buried. "I meant to place some flowers there."

"Griffiths would switch me good if he found me wasting time as he puts it."

"You work harder than any lad I know."

"The tavern's full again and it's only the forenoon. On account of the wind, I reckon."

She looked out the nearest window where pewter clouds scudded across a darkening sky and promised a thunderstorm. Despite the protective presence of so many guests, she couldn't rid herself of the dread of Griffiths' threats because she was well convinced he was entirely capable of inflicting them.

He had timed his return carefully. Not too early to rouse a man muddled by drink. Not too late lest he find Griffiths irretrievably into cards and surrounded by bad company. Mid-afternoon, Bleu approached the crossroads to the tavern and found it overflowing if the folks on the grounds and porch were any indication.

Given he didn't mean to stay long, it didn't matter.

Clouds hung heavy and distant thunder mimicked a panther's growl to the east. When he came into the tavern's yard beneath its wind-rustled trees he expected Titus to run out and greet him, seeing to the horses, no doubt asking why there were two instead of just Windigo. When that didn't happen, Bleu did the deed himself, wondering what he'd find when he entered the tavern as the stables were full.

Once past the crowded porch and inside the passageway, he removed his cocked hat in anticipation of Brielle. Confined to the kitchen, he guessed. Despite his rather mercenary mission, he couldn't deny his swelling need to make sure she'd come to no harm in his absence. He knew men and Griffiths was among the worst of the breed. Crass, unpredictable, grasping. Capable of unspeakable things.

Men and women eyed him as they entered and exited the public rooms and went up and down the stairs. Something smelled burnt. He saw Titus serving first one table then the next, a harried look on his face. Had he no help? Bleu continued walking toward Griffiths' office, surprised to find him there. A man—one of the hired guards he remembered—stood by the fireless hearth. The airless room was rife with ill feeling.

Bleu exchanged a hard, wordless look with the guard who went out.

Standing, Griffiths remained behind his desk. "What brings you back here, Galant?"

"A business matter." Bleu moved into the room and shut the door.

"Be quick about it. The tavern is bursting and I've little time to waste."

Bleu tossed the leather pouch he'd been carrying onto the cluttered desk. "I've come for your two indentures. Miss Farrow and Titus Owens."

Surprise flashed across Griffiths' sweaty face as his hand shot out to finger the offering.

"Spanish dollars," Bleu told him. "Pieces of eight."

Griffiths smirked. "The woman and boy are hardly worth that."

"They're worth a great deal more."

"I can't part with them." He let go, the coins clinking. "I've no other help at present."

"Tell your guards to make themselves useful." Bleu's gaze traveled to the cracked window and saw another hired gun near the stables. "It's a fair deal and you need the money."

Griffiths stiffened. "How would you know?"

"I've just come from Winchester where I confirmed that you are the late Griffiths' heir despite my doubts. You're a wanted man, *monsieur*. Wanted, in fact, across much of Virginia but somehow your gambling and thieving haven't caught up with you."

For a trice Griffiths' ire faded to alarm.

"Your debts are many, addicted to dice and drink as you are," Bleu continued. "There's a new debtor's jail beside the Winchester courthouse. Perhaps now would be the time for me to post an advertisement in Virginia papers telling your creditors of your whereabouts. Once that becomes known you'll have neither tavern nor indentures."

Bleu reached for the pouch, half-amused when Griffiths seized it with a cat-like swipe. "Take your indentures and get out of my sight."

"Count the coins and write down our arrangement." Inking the quill on the desk, Bleu extended it. "I'll tell Miss Farrow and the boy they're free."

He couldn't keep the mockery from his tone nor tamp down his soaring elation. Leaving the office, he sought the kitchen and found it empty though plenty of pots and pans spat and burbled in the hearth. The back door was open wide as if the Sabbath raid that dark day had never happened.

He stepped outside as another growl of thunder came from the east and the sun hid behind a bank of clouds. Somehow it seemed fitting to find Brielle in the garden for that was his shining memory of her. Surrounded by beauty. Trying to hold tight to something lovely amid the turmoil. Her back was to him as she bent and picked mint hurriedly, adding it to her basket. Had she run out of the mint punch the tavern served?

At so mountainous a moment he reverted to the language nearest his heart.

"*Venez, nous partons.*"

Come, we are leaving.

She whirled around, upsetting her basket and staring at him as if he was a phantom. He held out a hand, savoring the sudden joy in her expression. And then she burst into tears, her hands covering her face as her shoulders shook with silents sobs. He'd seen his sister, Sylvie, do the same when overcome and she had no words.

He set down his gun, retrieving the basket at her feet—and the spilled mint—though she had no need of it now. His own eyes were damp, and he wanted nothing more than to put his arms around her till her emotional storm quieted. As it was, on one knee before her, he handed her the basket when she lowered her hands and looked at him again.

"Please repeat to me what you said." A dozen questions clouded her eyes. "I think I misunderstood."

Brielle looked at Bleu, every inch of her wanting his embrace if only to steady her. His sudden appearing turned her to jelly, her shock at seeing him eclipsed by his more shocking words.

Come, we are leaving.

We? Other than the trinity, never had there been a more blessed *we*, at least to her.

She stared at him, afraid to hope what she'd heard was true. His intensity told her there was much more. "We're leaving here together—you, me, and Titus. Your freedom has been paid for, your contracts fulfilled. Griffiths is signing the transaction now. All that needs doing is gathering your belongings."

Taking back her dropped herb basket, she tried to make sense of what he just said. What sort of man bought one's freedom? Freedom for the both of them couldn't have come cheap. Why had he done so?

"Titus was last in the public room." The boom of thunder jarred her into action. "I'll collect what we have from the attic."

The satisfaction in Bleu's expression—the feeling in his eyes—was something she'd need to unravel in time. For now, an urgency to depart overtook her, as if Griffiths might change his mind and freedom was fleeting. She all but ran up the back stair to the attic. Her belongings—and Titus's—were blessed few. In her haste she nearly forgot her most beloved possession, her mother's jewelry box. Wrapping it in a petticoat, she safeguarded it for travel.

Taking a deep breath, she tried to quiet her emotions as she returned downstairs. This morning's confrontation with her former bondsman had lost its power. The iron bolt still lay on the kitchen table.

Bleu's return seemed nothing short of providential.

12

$\mathcal{B}$leu walked toward the stables as lightning slashed the sky. Folks dispersed in all directions, seeking shelter as the wind picked up and nearly removed his felt hat. Titus had seen him and come out of the tavern at a near run as if Bleu might leave before he could speak with him.

"I never thought to see you again." The boy's eyes rounded, his pleasure plain. "What brings you back?

Bleu tousled his shock of flaxen hair. "Your work here is done. Follow me to the stables and I'll tell you more."

In a quarter of an hour the three of them had filled saddlebags with their meagre possessions as well as provisions for the journey, Griffiths' signed paper secured. They said little as they prepared to go, caught in a web of shared joy and disbelief. Neither the weather nor the unknown could diminish the triumph of the moment.

"She's sure a fine horse." Titus ran a hand over the newly shod roan Bleu had bought as Brielle looked on. "I've never seen such trappings."

The woman's saddle had a fine slipcover of blue cloth. With Brielle in mind, he'd paid handsomely for both in Winchester. The timely purchase had restored some of his hard-won peace and somehow seemed confirmation of his plan to redeem them.

After visiting Tamsen's gravesite a final time, Bleu handed Brielle up, sensing her quiet astonishment. Titus sat on a second pillion saddle behind her. He made sure they were comfortable before securing his rifle and mounting Windigo. He cast an assessing glance at the glowering skies and led out, intent on caverns a few miles distant that might shelter them from the worst of the weather.

He kept his gaze on the shifting landscape, not Brielle, lest he be less than vigilant. The Indians had struck too recently for ease and though he'd encountered no sign since, he felt it was only a matter of time till another raid bloodied the valley.

Brielle and Titus rode silently behind him as one mile stretched to two. With every plodding step he felt relief, if not for himself, for them. He didn't know much of their past or the hardships they'd suffered. All he knew was that their paths had inexplicably crossed, and he'd felt driven to do something to help them.

The thin trail cut to the left and wound upwards past thickets of wild berries and mountain laurel. Expelling a tense breath, he removed his hat and tucked it under a saddle strap as a cool wind bestirred the woods. Looking back over his shoulder at them, he pressed on toward the entrance to a cavern, damp air rolling over them as they neared the cave's mouth. He helped Brielle down from the roan and then Titus slipped to the ground on his own.

"A cave?" he exclaimed, wide-eyed again as rain began spattering down. "In the nick of time, too!"

"There's another world beneath our feet but we won't go further than the entrance," Bleu cautioned, leading the horses beneath a wide ledge. "I wouldn't even hazard it with a lantern but it makes a fine shelter."

And so they rested in the cave's cool embrace, not speaking but waiting till the weather quieted. Once it did, they continued on, not passing another living soul, just forest creatures who were slowly reappearing after the drenching, songbirds foremost.

"Soon we'll come to another wonder," Bleu told them with a slight smile. "There's a reason I travel this way and bypass your former crossroads."

If she'd not lost her heart to him yet, the fiery sunset and the hot springs sheltered by tall, leafy sycamores would have done it. Still stunned by the day's events, Brielle removed one of her shoes and worn stockings and dipped a foot into a pool of steaming water. To allow her privacy, Titus and Bleu had gone further down the wooded hill where another larger pool waited. She was alone, her body sore after untold miles of riding though her spirits soared like the hawk above them.

She finished undressing, wanting to burn her work garments, wishing she had a comely dress and smallclothes. Sighing in delight, she sank below the water as steam hazed the woods around her. She could hear Titus talking to Bleu in the distance, a reassuring sound as twilight crept in and fireflies flashed.

All the questions she'd tucked away when he'd surprised her in the garden had been building but she was too tired to give them voice. Their supper had consisted of ham and the wheaten bread and cheese she'd taken from the tavern kitchen. Now, at the springs, she knew sleep would soon follow. For now it was enough that they were far from the tavern, walking in freedom.

Her questions would wait.

At daybreak, Brielle rolled up the striped woolen blanket that had made a far better bed than her attic mattress. Titus was at the hot springs again while Bleu readied the horses for another day's journey. She watched him unawares, his back to her. Just how far had they come from the tavern? Already its familiarity was fading, further clouded by the wonders unfolding around them. She hadn't looked back when they left. She didn't want to remember any of it, only what stretched before her.

"How did you sleep?" he asked when she approached. "Rather, did you?"

She smiled as wonder tied her tongue. How she wished she could speak her mind. Her heart.

I dreamt a handsome stranger saved me.

"That's the softest bed I've had since Philadelphia, thank you."

"You'll trade it for a feather mattress once we reach Orchard Rest."

"Your sister's home."

He knelt and filled a canteen from a cold spring gushing from a limestone ledge. "Sylvie has lived along the Rivanna since the Seven Years' War began."

"She came from Canada, like you?"

"*Oui*, a long, tumultuous story. *Tragique*. I will let her tell you in time." His eyes met hers again. "And I would hear yours."

She felt a sudden shyness. Rarely did anyone ask about her past. She didn't want to delay them with conversation, but Titus was exploring the woods and Bleu showed no sign of being in a hurry.

"I'll tell you the short of it," she began, smoothing her wrinkled petticoat. "My father was from a family of English saddlers in the West Midlands. England. He met my mother when he traveled to France to deliver a saddle and accoutrements to her father, a count, who was against their courtship. When they eloped to England he threatened to come after her, so she and my father sailed to the colonies. They settled in Philadelphia where Father resumed his trade ..."

"As a saddler?"

She nodded. "I was born in the city, and we lived happily there till I was sixteen and they died of a fever."

His eyes clouded. Were his and his sister's losses much the same?

"Since I had no kin in the colonies, I went to the city's Alms House for a time." A long time. But even that had been preferable to indentured servitude. She was still able to attend church and walk past her parents' former house in the city. And she'd been assigned the task of teaching other orphans to read and write.

He stood. "Did your family have no friends who would take you in?"

She hesitated. Here was the question she dreaded—and where her story became especially hard to tell. "I spoke little English, mostly French. The two families who considered taking me in decided not to."

"Did they say why?"

Till now she'd never told another soul. But she wanted nothing but truth between them. She owed him that after all he'd done for her. "It was thought I'd attract undue attention in their households and cause ... unrest."

Understanding struck his eyes.

She looked away. "Eventually, I was taken from the city's Alms House and contracted to Griffiths who left Philadelphia for Virginia ..." She took a breath, her shame shifting to joy. "And then, like something out of a fairytale, I was rescued by a Métis frontiersman from Acadie."

He smiled and handed her the canteen. "A Métis frontiersman who is determined to give *Madame Royale* a *joyeux* ending."

"You are too kind," she said, all a-fumble again. She took a long, thirsty drink, spilling water down her bodice and feeling nothing like *Madame Royale*. "'Tis too grand."

"You are the granddaughter of a *comte*, no?"

"That seems another world." Still, she'd oft wondered about the French family on another continent she'd never met. *Maman* had written her estranged father letters. Whether or not he'd replied escaped her. Then and now the past gnawed at her but she had no answers.

Bleu's mesmerizing gaze returned to her as she handed him the canteen. "Have you ever wanted to sail there ... to France?"

She hesitated. How could she answer when she'd never considered the possibility? She just lifted her shoulders slightly.

"I knew there was something different about you," he murmured before turning away as Titus approached and showed him an arrowhead he'd found.

Something different?

She prayed whatever he saw in her was *bon*. As *bon* as what she saw in him. The more time she spent with him, the more aware she was of her history. Even her long-discarded French revived.

"I've never seen the like of those hot springs," Titus said, tucking the arrowhead in his pocket, his voice alive with wonder. "What's the Rivanna River like?"

"The Rivanna is colder. Made for ferrying and fishing." Bleu turned toward Brielle, helping her into the saddle and hefting Titus up after her. "You'll find plenty to do living alongside it if you don't drown."

Titus grinned as Brielle took a last, fleeting look at the place that had made a lasting memory. Atop Windigo, Bleu led out again and her view narrowed to her roan's velvety ears and just beyond it. She was becoming used to all the lines and contours of him astride. Back straight, his dark hair caught in a leather tie that fell between squared shoulders, he rode almost effortlessly, a striking blend of balance and command.

She felt clumsy in comparison though the saddle was extraordinarily well made, even comfortable, and Titus made no complaint riding behind her. Somehow they sensed they needed to be quiet. Talking was reserved for mornings and evenings out of the saddle. Caution became their watchword. Thankfully, the further east they traveled the less the danger, Bleu had told them.

As they rode through deep green woods and flowering thickets, past high-as-the-heavens waterfalls spilling over clifftops, and up and down steep ridges teeming with creatures large and small, she had no cause for complaint. It put them further from the *Rose and Crown* and the diminished life they'd led there.

That night once they'd washed at a rushing creek and partaken of a cold supper, Titus fell asleep atop his blanket roll. Across from her, Bleu leaned back against the trunk of an oak, Mohawk pipe in hand, the fragrant tobacco whitening the air between them.

Though drowsy, she'd rather savor her surroundings and his company than sleep. In the last of the light she sat and mended Titus's torn breeches with the sewing kit she'd brought. "So, now that you know my story," she began quietly, "when will you tell me yours?"

"My story?" Though she didn't look up she sensed he smiled. "Perhaps it's better left untold."

"I would hear every bit of it, even the hard parts," she said, her stitches hurried as darkness rushed in.

"We have much in common. Is that not enough?" he replied. "We are both homeless. Unwed. Without work. Attached to a child not our own."

"There is much more to you than that."

He chuckled and took another draw on his pipe. "I will give you the short of it as you said."

Would he? What she wanted was the long of it, too. Looking up, she saw stars winking, the moon a mere crescent as it rose. She continued her mending though she was tempted to stop what she was doing and focus fully on him. Modesty kept her from it. Perhaps it was easier to speak freely unobserved?

"I was born in Acadie, as you know," he began. "My French father, Gabriel Galant, was head of our clan there. My Mi'kmaq mother died before I could walk, and he remarried an Acadian woman. I spent a great deal of time with my mother's people and learned their ways well. I also spent time with my half-sisters and half-brothers—Sylvie, Pascal, Lucien, and Marie-Madeleine— until the great upheaval happened."

"The expulsion when the British invaded and took your lands."

"*Oui, le Grand Dérangement.*" He paused and she held her breath.

Was the subject too sore?

"I recall displaced Acadians arriving in Philadelphia and living on Pine Street." She set her sewing aside. "My mother and I attended St. Joseph's Church on William's Alley where some of them worshipped and even wed."

"More than a few landed in Philadelphia, *oui,* while the Galants and their kin were scattered to the winds. Only Sylvie and I survived—or so we believe. Our brothers tried to flee and avoid exile. We don't know their fate. My Acadian mother and father and young sister were lost at sea."

So many losses. "And you?"

"I had been working for Hudson's Bay Company till the war began but most of my time was spent as a Resistance fighter against the British and their allies."

"I sensed you are a warrior most of all. Your scar tells me so."

"A warrior? Those days are behind me, and I am not proud of all that I did." Regret weighted his words. "In the fight I nearly took the life of the man who became my brother-in-law—a British officer."

She paused, sensing more violence he'd left unsaid. "How did you come from Canada to the American back country? To Fort Pitt?"

"With the war full-blown I became an interpreter and guide, a liaison between the tribes and colonial governments and military. That has kept me engaged the past eight years. Now that the British have pushed back the French I might continue that work, but for the moment I am free to visit Virginia and my sister again."

She felt a qualm for the first time as the repercussions of what he'd done set in. "With two strangers dogging your steps."

"I never expected to fall into so fortunate a circumstance, *non*." The amusement in his voice returned and she sensed they were on safer ground, a step away from any raw memories. "My sister will be delighted with your company. She can even sew us all new garments."

More abundance. More gifts. Brielle looked to her skirt's hem torn by brambles. Was Sylvie as generous as her brother?

"I don't want to be beholden to her—or you." Even now she was trying to think of ways to repay him in future though she had no work—no plan—

"I want no repayment if that is what you're thinking. Your presence is payment enough."

She looked up then but only saw the barest glimmer of him through the darkness, his pipe glowing like a star. "Why did you ... rescue us?"

The silence between them lengthened, so fraught with feeling she held her breath.

"It was in my power to do something and so I did," he finally said.

So simple an explanation for so grand and noble a gesture. She'd still not thanked him properly as words seemed woefully lacking ...

Even now she felt a flicker of fear, half expecting something dire to happen and ruin his heroic deed. She was not used to kindness. To honor. She hardly knew how to behave in the face of it.

"I hope you know how very grateful I am, Bleu Galant. I speak for Titus, too."

13

Soon they began to see fewer lone cabins in isolated clearings and more clusters of homes, grainfields and gristmills, even a small town or two. When they spent the night at an inn, the proprietor mistook them for a family.

"I have one empty room left for you and your wife and son, Mr. Galant."

A little thrill passed through Brielle. Even Titus seemed proud when Bleu didn't correct the assumption. Never mind that once Bleu had seen them safely to their lodging upstairs after a shared supper, he slept in the stable near their horses. Brielle lay down atop the unfamiliar mattress, a golden glow about her. It was enough to be thought of as Mrs. Galant for even a trice.

Week's end brought them to the headwaters of the Rivanna River which, Bleu explained, ran from Charlottesville to the James River for almost fifty miles. Its watery journey from the foothills onto the Piedmont plain made her realize how vast Virginia was. Their mutual relief was palpable to have come so far unhindered. They'd weathered the wilderness and summer heat with its swarms of biting mosquitoes and black flies unscathed.

When Brielle thought she couldn't go another step, Bleu pointed to a smudge of grey marring the horizon. "See the smoke from Orchard Rest's chimneys?"

Could it be? They hastened toward it, their horses closing the distance, the high voices of children carrying over fields and woods. Next they passed into an immense orchard with more fruit trees than Brielle had ever seen in one place. Countless apples and pears, peaches and cherries, soon to be theirs for the taking. A handsome stone house on a hill came into view as well as other buildings resembling what seemed more a village than a plantation.

Bleu dismounted behind a one-story cottage near rows of apple trees. Charmed, Brielle wondered who lived there as he helped her from the saddle. Tired of riding, Titus was already running toward the distant childish voices with a zeal that made her eyes fill. He'd rarely been around other children. She hoped he'd meet lifelong friends.

Turning back to Bleu, she watched him hobble the horses. Through the trees lay the glint of a river. Suddenly self-conscious, she looked down at her worn, torn linen, one shoe missing a heel.

"As I said," he reassured, obviously noting her dismay, "Sylvie will soon get-up new garments for us both."

Taking her elbow, he started up the hill beneath the shade of full-grown oaks to Orchard Rest. A woman appeared in the doorway, joy etched across her face. Sylvie?

"*Bonjour, frère!*" she called, hurrying down the porch steps.

Smiling, Bleu quickened his pace and caught her up, swinging her round till her feet left the ground. Brielle looked down at the grass, not wanting to intrude on the tender moment.

"And who is this lovely creature?" Sylvie asked him, on her feet again, hope and surprise in her striking features.

"*C'est ma future épouse même si elle ne le sait pas encore,*" he answered quietly without hesitation. "*Mademoiselle* Gabrielle Farrow."

Though his rapid French eluded her his sister's outright wonder did not. Sylvie threw her arms about Brielle in a warmhearted embrace.

"Pleased to meet you, *Madame* Blackburn," Brielle said, warmth creeping up her neck as Bleu looked on.

"Please, call me Sylvie. And may I call you Gabrielle?"

"Brielle, thank you."

"*Très jolie.*" Sylvie turned back to her brother. "You've come far from the look of you. Hurry inside and let me feed you before the children discover you've returned. They've been playing down by the river on so warm a day."

"We have a young boy traveling with us." Bleu looked down the hill to the heavily treed riverbank. "I suspect he'll soon find your tribe and make introductions."

"Then he'll be welcomed warmly." Sylvie led them into the house and a cool, shadowed hall. "Will is away surveying. Before he left we had a small feast and roast *porc.* There's plenty left over."

"Providential timing," Bleu told her, hanging his cocked hat from a wall peg.

"And after that a bath and new clothes."

"You have both waiting, I presume?"

"I am always hopeful of your arrival so I prepare, *oui.* And since I am forever sewing for the settlement, there are plenty of women's smallclothes and gowns to choose from, too," she added with a smile at Brielle.

They followed her through a dining room into a spacious kitchen with whitewashed walls and abundant cupboards. "Please, have a seat and let me serve you. Cider, to start?"

In a quarter of an hour they'd finished the bountiful meal including refills of the delicious cider as Sylvie sat at the table with them. "Much has changed since you were here last year. More Acadians have joined us and others have gone further south to the new community in *Louisiane*. Thankfully the winter and spring were mild. Our only woe was when lightning struck and one of the barns burned. But the wheat yields have been the best since we first began fieldwork years ago."

"Your orchards are thriving," Bleu told her, setting down his fork.

"The cider apples especially. Our larders are bursting from season to season." Sylvie began clearing away dishes. "Now, are you ready for a bath? Some rest?"

When Sylvie declined her help cleaning up, Brielle turned her attention to making herself presentable. Hot water was hauled upstairs to a copper tub in a bedchamber. Left alone, she could hear Bleu and Sylvie talking downstairs, still in the kitchen.

As she parted with her begrimed clothes she took in the lovely room, the canopied bed hung with yellow curtains that matched the fabric at the windows. Window seats overlooked a walled garden at the back of the house that reminded her of her parents' in Philadelphia.

Sylvie soon reappeared with garments, not just one dress and petticoats but several, reminding her that Bleu had told her his sister had been a seamstress in Acadie before the expulsion. She'd even worked at the Governor's Palace in Williamsburg for the governor's wife and daughters. And now, all of this.

The tub was emptied quickly and whisked away to be refilled for Bleu.

"I could more easily bathe in the river," she overheard him say to his sister's protests across the landing.

"*Bof!*" she rebuked him. "You are in civilization now, not the wilds like a beast."

Another door shut, ending the matter, and Brielle stood in a newly made linen shift and boned stays, fingering a chintz petticoat draped across the bed, her washed hair hanging to her hips. Sylvie

Galant Blackburn was not only gracious but also exceptionally skilled. Expert tiny stitches and seams, pleats and embellishments elevated every garment. Numerous pins studded a pincushion awaiting all the pinning required to encase her in the gown of her choice. Everything was hers, Sylvie told her, including clocked stockings, even an assortment of shoes.

Left alone, Brielle wondered the significance of such extravagance. Though Bleu had assured her of his sister's hospitality, she hadn't expected to be treated like family. Dare she say it?

Almost like a bride.

Bleu stood at the bottom of the staircase as Brielle came down, her hand on the banister, her eyes on him. No one else was in the hall in a hard-won moment that left him speechless. To his sister's credit, he no longer smelled of sweat and horses but rosemary soap and freshly laundered linen. As for Brielle, she hardly resembled the same woman who'd gone upstairs an hour before, making him realize the rigors of the trail had not been easy on her. Though her hair was still damp it had been pinned up simply but alluringly, her skin aglow, her gown a work of art.

He gave a slight bow which made her smile. She cleared the bottom step and stood looking up at him. He fisted his hands to keep from touching her. His pained restraint was short lived as the front door burst open behind him and half a dozen children rushed in.

"*Oncle* Bleu!" Childish voices echoed in the wide hall as his nieces and nephews danced around them and eyed Brielle with sharp interest. "*Oncle* Bleu!"

He saw Sylvie's attention dart to the open doorway where a thoroughly wet Titus stood, looking elated yet sheepish. He'd found the river to his liking. Perhaps that sufficed for a bath.

"You're finally here!" the children piped. "How long will you stay?"

"*Calme,*" he told them, embracing them like he wanted to do Brielle. "Introduce yourselves to *Mademoiselle* Farrow first."

The girls curtsied charmingly while the boys mimicked his previous bow. Suddenly quiet, they looked to Brielle as if waiting for her to release them from the polite silence.

"Tell me your names," she said with a smile.

Oldest to youngest, they obliged.

"I shan't remember at first so you'll have to help me," she told them, repeating each. "Madeleine, Talbot, Morgan, Amélie, Jolie, and Corbin."

"There's another *bébé* coming at harvesttime," Madeleine announced as Sylvie left the kitchen and joined them. "Right, *Maman?*"

Sylvie nodded. "*Garçon* or *fille* ... which will it be?"

"Boy," Corbin, the eldest, said confidently. He'd grown a foot since last meeting. "And his name must be Bleu."

"*Non,* a girl!" Amélie insisted, her freckled face pink. "*Primevère!*"

"Primrose?" Bleu asked. "What sort of *absurdité* is that?"

The girls giggled and the boys groaned as Bleu motioned for Titus to join them, dripping water and all.

"I hope you will be especially kind to our guests," Sylvie told them, inviting Titus to eat in the kitchen. "They have come a long way and need rest."

Madeleine laced her arm through her uncle's. "Will you stay in the cottage or here in the house? I ask because *Maman* had the cottage redone and even papered the walls. I think Miss Farrow would find it quite nice."

Bleu winked at his nieces and nephews. "We'll decide who is to be where once we weather the storm of you."

14

That night on Sylvie's porch, Bleu looked down on the cottage where Brielle had settled with Titus, the windows framed in candlelight. Alone with his sister on the porch, the children abed, he felt a rare contentment creep in, rubbing away the calluses of the outside world.

"So what do you think of Miss Farrow?" he asked, his voice so low he didn't think his sister heard him as it took her a moment to answer.

"She's lovely—astonishingly so," Sylvie told him in low tones. "And I have a great many questions."

"You've recovered from the shock of our arrival?"

"What I haven't recovered from are your words to me at introduction."

"When I told you she is my future bride but may not know it yet?"

"Exactly."

"Given we met so recently, I would give her time."

"I don't think she needs time. Her every look at you tells a different story."

Did it? Uncertain, he shifted in his chair though his eyes didn't leave the cottage.

"And I see how you look at her ..." She leaned in as if aware they might be overheard. "Tell me why, when no other woman has ever turned your head, you have suddenly lost your head to someone you've only known briefly?"

He lifted his shoulders, the mystery beyond him. "Some might say it was a bad beginning." Though he didn't like to remember that black Sabbath, he told her about the raid and Sylvie's delight changed to dismay. "When I first saw her she was lying on the ground and I thought she was among the dead."

"She'd fainted?"

He nodded. "Despite everything, when she came to and looked at me it was like lightning." He remembered the charged moment so vividly it was like reliving it all over again. "It doesn't hurt that she is, as you said, astonishingly *belle*. But it goes far beyond that."

"How so?"

"When I am with her ..." He paused, trying to corral words when he had none. "When I am with her I feel I've come home. It's as if I've wandered for many years without a compass or map and have finally found what I've sought. I never thought it would be a person but a place. But it is very much a person, and I cannot explain it any better than that."

"You're in love with her."

"I am hardly a worthy prospect."

"You settled her indenture contract," she reminded him. "What other recommendation or gallant gesture is needed?"

"I don't want her to wed me because she feels indebted. That may be her mind at present, clouding her judgment. For now she is liberated and sees me as her hero. I'll just enjoy that for however long it lasts."

Sylvie laughed softly and he felt encircled by the warm family feeling he'd missed. He had no confidante other than his sister ... till Brielle. Theirs was a newfound intimacy he didn't even know he needed, filling up the hollow places he'd long had inside him.

"You've prayed about her?" she asked.

Had he? His endless roaming, his longing for home, seemed a plea or prayer in itself. Since leaving Fort Pitt, caught up in events he'd not foreseen, he'd hardly been heavenly minded. But since some prayers went unanswered didn't it stand to reason some were answered unasked?

Sylvie continued quietly. "I've not stopped praying for you and your future bride since leaving Acadie. You'll make a fine husband and father. I've thought so for a long time now."

"I am without work, a means to sustain her."

"You've not lacked work since the war began."

His thoughts whirled backwards instead of forwards. "Once I accused you of provisioning the enemy when your husband, the infamous Blackburn, first came to our door. Would you have me do the same?"

She wafted her fan so vigorously he felt its wind. "What means you?"

"I've had offers from the British—colonial governors of Virginia and Pennsylvania—to continue acting as official interpreter and guide."

"Yet you can't sustain a bride?" Her voice held disbelief. "Do they pay so little?"

"Two hundred pounds sterling a year."

She gasped. "Are you jesting? 'Tis a small fortune!"

"The Lords of Trade are wanting to establish good relations with the tribes now that peace has been declared. A precarious path of coercion and exploitation."

"Then I shan't offer my congratulations."

"*Non.* Payment aside, I have little peace about the position."

"You still consider England the enemy."

"Our forced removal from Acadie is not easily forgiven nor forgotten."

"For a long time I felt like you. I still do though my ire doesn't burn as bright. I've only moved past it by choosing a new life here and letting the past rest."

"Marrying the enemy didn't hurt," he jested.

She smiled. "He's Scots, he often reminds me, not English."

"When will he return?"

"One never knows with surveying. He's not far, just north of Charlottesville, a safer survey unlike forays into the back settlements." Her voice tightened with concern. "I wonder, given the recent raid sparing Brielle and Titus, if that whole territory won't soon be ablaze again."

He nodded. "Western Virginia remains a ring of fire but at least I don't have to watch my back here. The Rivanna is incredibly civilized."

She sighed. "I suppose it's too soon to start sewing Brielle's *trousseau*."

"Sew all you like, just don't announce it." He watched as the lights went out in the cottage.

How did one go about the business of courting when it hadn't been done before?

Brielle came awake wondering where she was before her thoughts swung to Bleu. Sunlight streamed across the cottage's pine plank floor, and she realized she'd slept later than she meant to. Titus snored faintly in the adjoining room, familiar and reassuring. He needed his rest. The featherbed Bleu promised had lulled them both into a sound night's sleep.

She lay still, reflecting on all that had happened since leaving the *Rose and Crown*. Her new lodging was as pleasing as her former attic had been plain. The Galants had spared no effort or expense at creating a welcoming bower down to the dove grey and rose wallpaper with matching bedding and the simple but well-made furnishings.

"I lived here before my marriage and now it's kept ready for guests who happen by," Sylvie had told her. "A place of happy memories and new beginnings."

In a quarter of an hour Brielle had managed her front-lacing stays and chosen a simple sage green gown and white linen apron rather than the fancy chintz of yesterday. Her braided hair was half hidden beneath a lace-edged cap, and she felt more herself than she had in years. Though her stomach rumbled hungrily, all she wanted was Bleu.

Stepping onto the unfamiliar porch had her looking everywhere at once. June had stolen May's apple blossoms and turned the sprawling orchard a lush green. She spied a footpath leading somewhere. To the heart of the settlement? The big house—Orchard Rest—seemed quiet. Was Bleu still abed upstairs?

She stepped off the porch and followed the path through the woods, unsure where it would lead her or who she'd meet. Yet she felt safe. Fully alive. Not having her day hemmed in with endless tavern tasks seemed a miracle. To her left, the Rivanna flowed southeasterly. When she'd come through the trees she saw the ferry Bleu had spoken of mid-river. A number of dependencies and outbuildings stood sturdily along both riverbanks.

On her side of the river, a wide lane divided smithy and stables from what looked to be a weaving house and dye shed. She counted a dozen weatherboard buildings painted a deep red and yellow. Men and women went about their work, none noticing her as she stopped at the wood's edge.

"*Bonjour, Mademoiselle Farrow.*"

The low, beloved voice turned her around. Out of buckskins and minus his weapons, freshly shaven and clad in breeches and boots and a linen shirt, Bleu looked entirely different yet every bit as handsome.

In his extended hand were wild strawberries. "For you."

"*Salut toi*." She took them with an exclamation of delight, feeding him one before eating the rest. "*Merci*," she added, the words pulled from some past part of her she'd thought lost forever.

His eyes held a question. "Would you like a tour of the settlement?"

At her nod they fell into step together, walking to one side of the dusty lane to avoid a passing wagon. The driver raised his hat to them, calling out a greeting.

"Do you know everyone?" she asked.

"*Non*." He took her arm and led her around a rut. "Some Acadians are new to me though many have been here since the settlement's founding eight years ago."

She soon lost count of the buildings he pointed out. Stillroom. Wash house. Stables. Smokehouse. Spinning house. Salt house. Even a communal dining room and kitchen. Barns stood in distant fields crisscrossed with rail fences. But it was the chapel in the bend of the river at the farthest end of the settlement that stole her attention and her heart. Modest and whitewashed, it boasted a steep, shingled roof and tall windows, the door affixed with decorative iron hardware.

"Small," she exclaimed when they stepped inside. "Yet well made."

"It serves many purposes," he told her as they walked the center aisle toward the altar. "Traveling preachers come by on occasion. Weddings and baptisms and christenings are celebrated—and sometimes funerals. There's even been talk of adding a bell tower."

The fenced cemetery she'd seen behind the chapel turned her melancholy, yet the quaint building held the peace she'd often craved. Her fears that her freedom would fall apart—that Griffiths would find her and Titus and return them to the tavern—lessened here. Though she knew it was senseless, trusting Bleu had taken care of the matter, she still couldn't shake her unease.

"I've not been in a church since Philadelphia." Eyes on the altar, she sat down on a wooden pew. "And you?"

"I find God more outside these four walls than within."

"The Creator of hot springs and waterfalls and wild strawberries." She smiled, thankful for all they'd experienced in so short a time.

Thankful, too, he couldn't divine her hopes of a wedding in this hushed, hallowed place. If he asked her this very moment to marry him right here and now she would, his smile wooing her though that might not have been his intention. Seized with shyness, she looked to her aproned lap, as tongue-tied as she was enamored.

Gabrielle Galant.

15

Sensing Brielle's sudden disquiet, Bleu led her out of the church to walk around the settlement on the river path, weighing whether to take her across the river, too. The day would be ablaze by noon but for now all was cooler and shaded, the river a continual rush. They'd not gone far when two women came toward them, baskets dangling from their arms.

Geneviève Turcot and Eulalie Benoit?

Brielle seemed shy again, unsure of herself. Was she out of her depth because of their rapid French? Or her new surroundings?

"Bleu?" Eulalie called out. "Is that you?"

"At long last," he replied as their attention shifted to Brielle.

He knew what they were thinking. He always came to the Rivanna settlement alone. Rarely was he seen walking with any woman save his sister or his nieces. In the past he'd always avoided such, even Sylvie's subtle attempts at matchmaking. He made brief introductions, their curiosity apparent.

"Gabrielle Farrow?" Eulalie asked in Français. "Do you speak French?"

When Brielle hesitated, Bleu said, "She's unfamiliar with our French patois—our Acadian French."

Brielle said as if in apology. "I remember some of my mother's tongue, but English is what I know best."

"Are you visiting the Rivanna?" Geneviève asked in English, shifting her basket to her other arm. "Or will you stay on?"

Brielle hesitated and looked at Bleu.

"She comes from the Winchester area and has yet to decide," he said, hoping they wouldn't delve deeper.

"For now, I want to be of help here in the settlement," Brielle said quickly. "Learn where I'm most needed."

"Start in the garden, perhaps," Eulalie said at once. "Summer's harvesting and preserving and pickling keep us continually busy and shorthanded. The usual seasonal fevers take a toll. We'll not stop till winter starts."

"Since we feed so many year-round, we must put by as much as we can. And now that we have another masculine mouth to feed"—Geneviève smiled at Bleu—"our work is unending."

"Come," Eulalie said, linking arms with Brielle. "We'll show you the gardens. Acres and acres of vegetables, herbs, and flowers."

Bleu watched them go, needing to return to his own task in the stables but reluctant to part with her. He stood by the river, watching them walk away. And then his whole world righted when Brielle looked back at him over her shoulder and smiled.

That night they sat in Orchard Rest's dining room, Bleu taking Will's chair at the head of the table, Sylvie at the other end while Brielle sat with the children, three on one side and four on the other, including Titus. Jolie, only two, sat upon Brielle's lap, having taken a liking to her that was amusing to all and made her feel all the more welcome.

Dark haired like Sylvie, she was stout, a baby *beignet*, her eyes the same startling shade of Acadie Bleu as her uncle. In fact, Brielle saw Bleu in all their faces, especially his nephews.

"Papa?" Jolie said, pointing to her father's chair then looking up at Brielle as if she alone knew the answer.

"Papa will be home soon," Madeleine told her with the authority of an older sister. "This is your *Oncle* Bleu, remember, though you were just a baby when you first met."

Dinner was a delicious chicken *fricot,* followed by berry tart, and washed down with plenty of cider.

"An extra serving for you three," Sylvie told her guests, eyeing Bleu particularly. "I'm sure you've had no *tarte* since coming from Fort Pitt."

They all lingered at the table, their shared laughter and talk reminding Brielle what being part of a family was like. Here all was safety and security and contentment. When she offered to help with the dishes, Sylvie shook her head in mock surprise.

"No need. That is what daughters are for." Smiling, she whisked the empty tureen off the table while her older girls did the rest. "Perhaps my brother can show you the walled garden instead."

Bleu stood and Brielle met his eyes and accepted his silent invitation. Out the back door they went, down steps that led to a gravel path and a small, scrolled iron gate.

She went in ahead of him as he said, "You wouldn't recognize this piece of ground had you been here when Will bought it at auction."

The aged brick walls seemed a vial of perfume and contained countless flowers—lavender, phlox, bee balm, wisteria, and clematis to name a few. Bees and butterflies abounded. Overcome by the sight and scent, Brielle came to a halt by a trellised climbing rose and savored the moment.

"All this loveliness reminds me of Philadelphia. Papa used to take us to Bartram's Garden on the Schuylkill River." A rush of happy memories came to mind. "And *Maman* used to talk of the gardens from her girlhood in France. *Château de Chambord* and *Jardin des Tuileries* and *Chenonceau* …"

Picking a rose, he offered it to her. "And her father's house?"

A bit wistful, she took it and breathed in the exquisite scent no perfumer could duplicate. "*Château de Villandry.*"

For years she'd been unable to think of all she'd lost. But now, removed from the distraction of work and the need to simply survive, her mind seemed open to these hazy, half-forgotten things. At the same time, she wondered Bleu's thoughts while trying to navigate hers. His own losses were many, yet he never bemoaned them.

"Do you remember much of your past in Acadie?" she asked as they slowly walked the gravel paths. "Rather, do you want to remember?"

"For years I've tried to outrun the life I once lived. Dwelling on the past makes me *furieux*. At the same time there are things I don't want to forget." He stopped by a sundial. "It is … bittersweet."

"I understand. We should try to dwell on the good as Scripture says."

His smile returned in confirmation. "Like your company here and now."

Soon Brielle felt caught up in the whirlwind of settlement life along the Rivanna. Titus began helping Bleu at the stables managing the horses, while her mornings were spent in the settlement gardens where she worked nearly as hard as she had at the tavern. Their days started ahead of dawn before the summer sun wilted both them and the plants. Weeding, hoeing, harvesting, sorting, cleaning, drying, pickling, and cellaring filled her hours but with all of the fulfillment and none of the fear or fatigue of before. Shared work made a lighter burden.

Sylvie stole her away afternoons where they sewed in Orchard Rest's parlor or on the covered porch. Her daughters, all but petite Jolie who was napping, joined them, sewing with nimble fingers in mimicry of their seamstress mother.

As the days unspooled, Brielle was able to share pieces of her past. A good listener, Sylvie seemed the sister she'd never had. Always the conversation circled back to Bleu. Though she looked forward to his joining them at meals, he began to appear only half the time and she realized he sometimes ate with other Acadians in the communal dining room called the kitchen house.

"He has many friends in the settlement," Sylvie explained.

"Not only friends, *Maman*." Madeleine whispered conspiratorially. "Sabine."

Sabine?

Brielle felt a qualm as Sylvie and Madeleine exchanged glances. She kept sewing a shirt for Titus, unasked questions swirling. There was much to learn about these Acadians. Though they lived in the American colonies they'd retained many of their customs and traditions as best they could.

Would she find out next that Bleu had a sweetheart?

"Sabine Broussard's father fought in the Resistance with Bleu," Sylvie explained as if sensing her sudden unease. "He's called *Beausoleil*. Shining Sun. He was a light for our people at a very dark time. He tried valiantly to preserve our way of life. In fact, he never stopped fighting even when most of us were put on prison ships and sent away from Acadie. He's since been captured and is a prisoner in Halifax."

"Canada?" Brielle looked down the wooded hill toward the settlement. "But Sabine is here?"

"She came seeking refuge with other Acadians after I married Will. She's been waiting for her father's release ever since."

"Might Beausoleil come here then?"

"To see Sabine, perhaps." Sylvie threaded her needle with beeswax and began work on a petticoat. "But word is he has his sights set on a French colony in the Caribbean."

Brielle felt inexplicable relief ... if Sabine would go with him. Had this woman captured Bleu's heart like he'd captured hers? Agitated, she poked her finger then wiped the fleck of blood on her apron, wishing her wayward emotions were as easily managed.

"She is very fond of Bleu, as are a few other young women," Sylvie told her in low tones. "But he's always avoided any romantic entanglements."

Brielle's mounting misery ebbed though her stitches stayed crooked.

"I'm hoping he settles soon, marries, and starts a family." Sylvie looked up at her briefly. "I want him to be as happy as I've been. My wish is that he stay here. He would make a fine husband and father should that happen."

A fine husband and father, truly. Sylvie echoed what Brielle had pondered more than once since he'd ridden into their lives at the crossroads. Why did he avoid any romantic entanglements? He'd spoken of Sylvie's matchmaking with a patient amusement—and seemed to take pride in remaining free.

Might she, a mere tavern maid, sway him?

16

Sabine Broussard stood by the kitchen house door, arms akimbo and expression smug, just as she'd been when he'd last seen her. "I thought you'd never return and am overjoyed you've proved me wrong."

Bleu regarded the young woman he'd known for so long she seemed more sister, albeit a quarrelsome one. "For now, *oui*."

She surveyed him intently as if searching for another scar, another sign of the conflict which had kept them apart. "Promise me you'll remain."

"The Rivanna is a homecoming of sorts," he said, "though I'm never sure how long I'll stay."

Even as he uttered the well-worn phrase he saw that it had become an easy excuse. To be distant. Absent. To risk nothing of his heart. Brielle had, unwittingly, helped him realize that empty evasion.

"I have a proposal for you." Sabine walked with him into the kitchen house where a line snaked past a long table laden with food. "But first let's eat."

More wary than curious, Bleu filled his trencher with the garden's bounty, remembering Brielle's tireless work there. Fresh-caught gaspereau from the Rivanna was the meal's main-stay, fried to perfection. Titus, he remembered, had contributed to the catch. Seeking a breeze, Bleu sat down at a table near an open window.

Sabine took a seat on the bench across from him as his attention veered to the kitchen house's open door. Brielle entered, making him forget his full plate and Sabine's unspoken proposal completely. It was the first time she'd joined them here. Had she come seeking him and Titus?

Two Acadians—a blacksmith and carpenter—were talking to her, gesturing for her to go ahead of them in line. She accepted with a smile though that didn't end their attentions. They continued to talk to her, asking questions and drawing her into conversation. Watching, Bleu's resistance roared. He hardly heard Sabine across from him.

"So, since you are always traversing all over why not escort me to my father in Halifax?"

"Halifax?" Distracted as he was with Brielle, he groped for an answer. "The enemy's den?"

"Ha! All of Acadie is now that. But at least we are finally free to visit there unhindered and not be imprisoned or expelled all over again."

"I vowed never to return." Try as he might, anger still burned beneath his stoicism. The heat of it nearly stole his appetite.

"A reunion with my father might change your mind, *non*? I've not seen him in eight long years, nor have you." Determination hardened Sabine's features. "The British officials might be willing to release him were he to leave Canada for good."

"Far-fetched."

"Please, consider it."

"Do you know what you ask?" He raised his gaze in warning. "We would need a ship's passage. Even then the journey would be long. Dangerous. Once we arrive—if we survive—he might not be there."

"You don't want to return."

"I have no desire to see Acadie under British rule." He forked a bite of fish but didn't eat. "Nor your father their captive."

"Not even to reunite with him?" Sabine's face was nearly the color of her russet hair. "To help *me* reunite with him, the only kin I likely have left?"

"You have family in south *Louisiane*, so I've heard." His voice was firm as always when battling Sabine. "As for a guide, I have several contacts and can arrange an escort. But I cannot go with you."

She frowned and fell silent though he was sure she wasn't finished with the matter. Swallowing a bite, he looked over Sabine's shoulder to Brielle again. She was garnering too much attention. Why had she decided to dine here instead of Orchard Rest? At least there she was spared excessive notice. Even in plain linen she was a feast of femininity—and being a newcomer only added to her allure. Since leaving the tavern she'd begun to bloom, her stark slenderness already a memory.

Sabine raised her voice as if realizing who'd stolen his attention. "So what is this I hear about you returning to the Rivanna with a woman and child?"

"Both, *oui*." He was feeling strangely terse and short tempered, the meal unappetizing, the talk and laughter around them overloud. He'd grown too used to the silence of the woods.

Brielle was with Eulalie now, nearly to the food, when Titus caught up with her. Spying Bleu, he waved a hand. Bleu smiled, struck by how the boy had changed for the better in the short time he'd been here.

"Granted, not all the settlement is Acadian so they should fit in well enough if they're willing to work and cause no trouble," Sabine was saying. "You must introduce us."

When Titus took a seat beside them a few minutes later, Brielle followed. Setting down his utensils, Bleu made introductions.

"You're from the back settlements?" Sabine asked them. "A very *dangereux* place to be."

Titus and Brielle exchanged a glance as she said, "We worked at a tavern overmountain."

Surprise washed Sabine's face—and disdain. Being *la crème d'Acadie* and a Broussard, Sabine's pride in her own lineage had never been more apparent.

"Servants," Sabine said flatly, even dismissively.

"Don't be deceived. *Mademoiselle* Farrow is the granddaughter of the *Comte de Sancerre*," Bleu told her quietly, continuing his meal. "From France."

A hush followed as Sabine's scorn switched to disbelief. She looked at Bleu as if he was jesting but he paid her no attention, nor did Brielle elaborate though he sensed her own quiet pride. He resisted the impulse to look her way again. Her hold on him was like a leather tie, strong and unyielding, tethering them in ways he couldn't fathom.

"I'm glad we've come here," Titus was saying as he wielded his fork and ate like a man thrice his size. "I'd rather work along the Rivanna than anywhere else on earth."

"It is a good place, a safe place to be." Sabine smiled at him. "We need more youth like you to grow this settlement. As for you, Miss Farrow, what skills do you bring?"

"I'm willing to do whatever is needed and necessary," Brielle answered, meeting Sabine's dissecting gaze. "For now I'm working in the gardens and making garments for the settlement."

"I'm sure Sylvie has something to do with that. Her needle never stops." Sabine turned to Bleu. "And you? How are you spending your time?"

"I'm in the stables and pastureland, herding horses and cattle." Bleu took a drink of cider. "Soon I'll help sow the winter wheat."

"The livestock have increased considerably since you were last here though it will never equal the Galants' vast herd of horned cattle in Acadie," Sabine lamented. "I'm glad to see you still have Windigo—and a beautiful white roan."

"The roan is Miss Farrow's," Bleu replied, meeting Brielle's eyes.

Her roan?

Brielle stared at Bleu, his sudden generosity failing to make much of an impression. She was too caught up in the maelstrom of emotion at their table. Though everyone behaved properly and nothing amiss had been said, the feeling between her, Miss Broussard, and Bleu pulsed like a rapidly beating heart.

Had she interrupted a *tête-à-tête*?

That had not been her intent. Titus had simply asked her to join him for the midday meal and so she'd come, hoping to see Bleu as well. Lately he seemed more distant, working and spending time away from Orchard Rest, making her wonder if he needed time away from her, too. Now that he had brought her here, did he feel matters finished between them? They'd never discussed what would happen in future once they reached the Rivanna settlement.

"What is your roan called, Miss Farrow?"

Sabine Broussard's question rattled her. Did the handsome horse that carried her here have a name? She and Bleu had never discussed that either. Brielle gave him a questioning glance and finally said—

"Pearl." It was all she could think of at the moment. Her mother had loved pearls. She'd given Brielle a string of them for her twelfth birthday, but they'd been lost or stolen during the many moves she'd made since.

Sabine regarded her intently. "You must enjoy riding then."

"I've not had much time lately …"

"Bleu is an excellent horseman."

Brielle nodded. "One of the finest. The equal of my father, a saddler."

Bleu looked at her again, the warmth of his gaze adding to that pulsing feeling. She took another bite of the delicious fish, listening as Titus talked to the boy on the other side of him. But Sabine, who Brielle decided had a fervent passion for Bleu, was not done with the conversation.

"Will you stay here in the settlement long, Miss Farrow?"

Sabine's question seemed barbed—or was she only imagining it?

"I haven't thought much beyond this moment," Brielle said truthfully. "My coming here was a surprise—a very pleasant one—and for now I'm grateful to be a working guest."

"You are more than a guest," Bleu told her kindly, eyes on his plate as he finished his meal. "Already Sylvie considers you one of the family. The children, too. I'm sure Will shall feel the same once he returns."

Sabine's brows raised in question. "Is *Monsieur* Blackburn away surveying?"

"He's expected home any time," Bleu told her.

"Perhaps you could discuss my proposal with him since you are in doubt."

Proposal?

Brielle finished her meal in silence as Eulalie approached, asking Sabine a question about the stillroom. Was that her domain?

In a few minutes the kitchen house emptied as men and women returned to work. Bleu excused himself and Sabine followed while Brielle lingered at table with Titus who was talking excitedly about making weirs the Acadian way and how many fish had been caught of late.

"I'm proud of you for being so useful," Brielle told him, her heart as full as her stomach. "Your happiness here lends to my own."

17

$\mathcal{S}$ abine followed Bleu to the stables where he was no more inclined to talk than he'd been at table. But the Broussards had
always been notoriously stubborn and Sabine was no exception.

As he reached for a pitchfork and began tossing hay into feed-
ers, she said, "Miss Farrow raises a hundred queries."

"I know little about her myself," Bleu admitted, struck by the
truth of it.

"Is it true she's the granddaughter of a *comte*?"

"So she says. I have no reason to disbelieve her."

"Did you know that when you rescued her?"

So Sabine knew that little-discussed detail?

"If you mean did that fact play into my decision to help her,
non." He held his temper by a thread. "What do you mean by
rescue?"

"The boy—Titus—told someone you settled both their
indenture contracts and redeemed them."

"And if I did?"

"Granted, you've always been generous but this seems …
peculiar."

He halted, wiping his brow with his sleeve. "Placing happiness
in the heart of another is peculiar?"

"It is more than that," she said heatedly. "Much more."

He wouldn't deny it. Nor would he discuss it. He continued pitching hay but she circled and stood in front of him.

"You're in love with her …" Her features tightened. "I feel it!"

So the truth was laid bare. How many knew besides Sylvie and Sabine?

He held her gaze. "I confess, I am not made of ice."

Tears glittered in her eyes. "I have waited *years* for you."

"There has never been an understanding between us."

"*Non*, but I've continued to hope you would return my affections ever since you joined forces with my father years ago. I have long dreamed of an alliance between the Broussards and Galants."

"Once, perhaps, our families were renowned. Respected. As for the other matter, you cannot force affection." His bluntness seemed harsh but necessary. "What we have is an enduring friendship."

She batted away a horsefly, all the more exasperated. "I'll never be satisfied with such."

He chafed at the obvious. Sabine had ever been persistent, rarely showing restraint. That Broussard trait had helped fuel the Resistance but seemed misplaced here. "Then your mislaid affections will blind you to the one who can give you what I cannot."

Speechless, she stared at him and then, whirling away, she fled the stables. He stood motionless, breathing in his earthy surroundings amid the profound relief of her leaving.

"Bleu."

Brielle stood at the stables' entrance. Had she crossed paths with Sabine as she left? He set aside the pitchfork, glad her expression wasn't troubled or perplexed but serene.

"I don't mean to halt your work …" she began.

Her smile seemed a lanthorn, lighting her lovely features. That was certainly how he felt in her presence. Full of light, life.

She signaled the future. Sabine reminded him of the past—the darkness—all that had been lost.

"Let's leave all this earthiness behind." Touching her arm, he led her into the open, beyond the heavy scents of manure and fodder.

Unfit for a *comte's* granddaughter, he thought half in jest.

"Walk to the chapel with me," she said. "There's such peace there."

He felt it, too, though he'd given it little thought before. Was Sabine watching? She might well follow, impassioned as she was. Chary, he opened the chapel door and then left it ajar to admit fresh air. They sat where they had at first, facing the altar. Peaceful and private, a rarity in a swelling, sweltering settlement.

She looked down at her folded hands. "Miss Broussard said she asked you to return her to Acadie—Nova Scotia."

Sacré bleu. He nearly uttered the oath aloud. "I told her *non.*"

Brielle seemed relieved. Was that her concern? That he would leave the Rivanna? For a trice he feared she would confide some concern or tell him she was leaving, instead.

"I'm glad if only for selfish reasons." All the tension left him as she continued as calmly as Sabine had been riled. "I can't imagine being here without you. For the first time in a long time the future holds hope."

Hope. He felt it, too, a flicker rather than a flame but there nonetheless.

She continued, eyes on the altar, her lovely features pensive. "Some in the settlement have asked me my plans, if I'll stay or move on."

"You've only been here briefly. Perhaps it is too soon to decide."

She looked back at him, a question in her eyes. "What did you have in mind when you freed us from the tavern?"

"All I knew is that I couldn't leave you there." He looked down at the plank floor, feeling he was half drowning in the depth of her gaze. "And now that we're here I haven't once thought of leaving."

"Meaning you never stay long."

"Not long enough for my sister." Or Sabine.

"If you left and I couldn't go with you I couldn't stay here either."

He mulled her words, so forthright and riven with feeling. "You have Titus."

She hesitated. "But Titus isn't you."

"What are you saying, *ma chère?*" His quiet question unnerved even him.

She turned toward him slightly on the pew. "I feel I owe you an enormous debt I can't possibly repay."

"I want no repayment, understand. Your happiness is enough."

"Do you have any coin left after freeing two indentures and buying so fine a horse?"

"Pearl?" He chuckled at the impromptu name. "Money well spent. I have plenty left, *oui.*"

"Promise me that if you do go you'll give me plenty of notice."

"I promise." Yet the longer he stayed the more *enchanté* he grew with each passing day.

"I hope that I am of help—of service—here." She looked to her lap and her worn hands that bespoke a life she wasn't meant for. "Though I am a good gardener I am a clumsy seamstress when compared to your dear sister."

"When you doubt yourself remember who you are. A woman of many talents. Related to French royalty. Never forget it. I cannot." Her obvious puzzlement pushed him to explain. "When I first met you, even before I knew your background, I sensed something different about you. Something that defied your indenture."

She looked dismayed. "I am not one to put on airs."

"Not in the least. I'm speaking of a rare grace and refinement that is simply a part of who and what you are, the very fabric of your being."

Her half-smile was sad. "Little good it's done me."

"Perhaps you don't belong here. Have you any desire to return to France? To learn if your grandfather still lives?"

She looked to the altar as if it held answers. "Even if I wished to, he might no longer be living. If he is he might not want to see me since my mother broke his heart leaving long ago."

"But if he does?"

Her silence left him weighing his own motives. He wanted, with all that was in him, to hear she wanted to be nowhere but beside him. That France held no allure. That she'd found her home in him. But could he live with the knowledge that he'd kept her from her true family? Her beginnings? What if that other, distant life was what she was truly meant for?

He searched for a shred of wistfulness in her voice when she said, "I was born in America, remember. I've never set foot in France."

"But suppose a whole new world awaits you there?"

Their eyes met again, his bearing a challenge, hers clouded with doubt.

"There's much to consider." She reached out and squeezed his hand in friendship, but her expression remained clouded. "For now my newfound freedom is enough."

18

William Blackburn returned and everyone along the Rivanna seemed to rejoice, Sylvie foremost. He came over the rise to the settlement with his chain men and markers and Noir, the black hound who'd replaced the irreplaceable Bonami after old age took him.

Weary and muddied by a recent rain, Will was clearly in high spirits to be home. *Home*. Once again, Bleu mulled the word. Where was home to him?

Where was Brielle's?

Bleu stood at a distance as Will's brood rushed forward like they'd done him at his return. A loving father, he scooped Jolie up into his arms and carried her toward the big house as the rest of his children cavorted around him. Sylvie stood on the porch, her joy palpable.

As Bleu watched all the Blackburns enter Orchard Rest, Titus came up behind him. "Is that the British Ranger everybody here talks about?"

"William Blackburn, *oui*. A celebrated Scots soldier who fought against France but has since come to his senses. *Revenir à la raison*."

"I don't want to be a soldier." Titus's intensity reminded Bleu his father had died in the last war. "I want to live along the Rivanna forever. I just wish my sister was here, too."

"I understand, but she is in a far better, more beautiful place."

Titus nodded, still downcast as Bleu gestured west.

"Would you care to see my land? It lies in back of the orchard."

"The unfinished house on the hill?"

"*Oui*." Bleu began walking through the apple trees as Titus trotted alongside him, nearly matching his long stride. "One day you'll own your own land if you continue working here in the settlement."

"How did you come by yours?"

"A gift from my sister and Blackburn."

A generous ploy to ensnare me which never held much appeal till now.

Titus ran ahead of him, past rustling trees with dense shade to the sloping rise that offered a territorial view of bluish-tinted hills and valleys.

"Is this all yours?" Titus called as he circled one stalwart brick wall.

"*Oui*"—Bleu eyed the unfinished structure with renewed determination—"though it is far from done."

"May I go inside?" Titus was already up the steps, hovering on the unfinished porch.

"Of course—but watch out for roosting pigeons."

Titus disappeared from sight, leaving Bleu alone. All that needed doing seemed to shout at him. A front door begged hanging. Glass windows belonged in gaping frames. Rooms needed furniture. Carpenter he was not, though there were several fine Acadian woodworkers in the settlement. He came to a stop beneath an old oak, one of several surrounding the house like sentinels.

Titus reappeared, leaning out a window. "You should show Brielle."

Bleu crossed his arms. "Why so?"

"She lived in a brick house like this when she was young and happy."

Young and happy.

A potent combination. The remark reminded him of his own childhood, much the same. And what had he to show for it since? Years of fighting that had come to naught. Selling his services to the enemy in a bid for peace. And now? Nothing but this unfinished *maison*, an echo of his indecision.

"Do you think she'd like it?" Bleu asked, studying the house with fresh eyes.

Titus came to stand beside him, his gaze rising to the gable roof. "She used to say she missed her old brick house, so aye ... or *oui*."

Bleu chuckled. He'd almost used stone but was suddenly glad he'd chosen brick.

"I do miss it," came a familiar voice behind them.

Together they turned, Bleu as surprised by Brielle's sudden appearance as he was Titus hurrying down the hill to join his young friends by the river. She passed by him, going up the house's steps just as Titus had done. He felt a beat of uncertainty. The house was small, smaller than Orchard Rest. He'd thought to live here himself, alone, so had made it so. And yet it was a house that could easily be added onto ...

He followed her inside, wishing the staircase's handrail was finished. His desire to show her around and gain her approval gave him a bone-deep satisfaction. Delighted, she passed from the wide passageway to the parlor and then crisscrossed to the kitchen before returning, her hands on each side of the doorframe.

"Such a magnificent view!"

He stood behind her, wanting to place his hands about her waist and kiss the little bare spot at the nape of her neck below her upswept braid. Instead he simply savored being closer to her than he'd ever been since that first day when he'd carried her from the crossroads.

"Is this all yours?" she asked, turning round to face him.

"Mine, *oui*." What he wanted to say was … *ours*.

Ours and our children's and their children's. Forever and ever.

He didn't step back. He just looked down at her. They were a hands-breadth apart. She didn't look away, her eyes luminous … adoring. Or did he only imagine it? His own passionate regard of her nearly got the better of him.

She sighed but it was a contented rather than sad sound. "Much like our brick house in Philadelphia."

"Tell me more about it."

"*Une belle maison.* The foyer was tiled in a black and white fleur-de-lis and a winding stair reached the second floor. Halfway up there was a little alcove where a small porcelain angel from France rested. Papa liked to tease that the only angel he needed was *Maman* …" Her voice faltered and she turned toward the view again.

He swallowed past the knot in his own throat. "If she was anything like you I can see why he said so."

Back to him, she fell silent and he unclasped his hands and placed them on her linen-clad shoulders. Turned away she seemed less a temptation to take in his arms.

But only slightly.

The warmth of Bleu's hands on her shoulders seeped through her linen dress. His touch drove away any sadness and left her half-melting with the desire to be in his arms. For a few moments Brielle forgot why she'd come up the hill.

"Sylvie asked me to fetch you and Titus for supper," she finally remembered.

Bleu's delayed response told her supper was the furthest thing from his mind, too. "Are you hungry?"

She simply nodded. In truth, every meal around the Blackburn's table only made her hunger for a home of her own. They started down the hill in step as a dog barked in the distance. Noir? The hound was often with the children when Will wasn't surveying, Sylvie said.

Bleu's shout seemed to reach the entire settlement. "Titus!"

When Titus came running she reached for his hand, wishing they could go inside the unfinished house instead and fill the rooms with life and laughter. That desire grew tenfold when they walked into Orchard Rest's dining room and found Will at the head of the table, a smiling Sylvie at the other end, their children ringed around them.

Rather than feel they'd intruded or spoiled a family moment, all of the Blackburns greeted them noisily, pointing out two empty chairs side by side while Titus joined the boys opposite. Brielle darted a look at Bleu and wondered if he felt the same craving for family, a shared future. So far he'd given no indication he did. Wasn't the unfinished house proof?

"Sylvie has told me what brought you three to our door." Will began carving a large ham. "You arrived at a good time. Summer has never been so plentiful."

All the garden's bounty seemed to have found its way to the long table. Sylvie's baking was nearly as exemplary as her sewing. Not only were there biscuits but cornbread and an assortment of jams and jellies, pickles and preserves. No one rose from a Blackburn feast hungry.

"And your surveying expedition?" Bleu asked as dishes were passed. "Sylvie said you were in Albemarle County."

"Aye. Just when I think Virginia has little left to survey this side of the mountains I'm called out again." Will smiled. "But so long as I can return to this I've no complaints."

Brielle's thoughts turned toward the unfinished kitchen beyond the orchard. Memories of her parents' Philadelphia kitchen with its cream crockery and apple-green shelves, the warm hearth that never seemed to fade, the aroma of baked *canelé* with its custardy-burnt sugar goodness filled her thoughts.

She smiled at Titus across the table, his sunburnt cheeks full as he ate. Once again his happiness was her own. She'd long regarded him as a mother might, zealous for his wellbeing and happiness. He was growing before her eyes, an inch taller already.

Supper ended with the older girls washing the dishes and the boys hastening outside for their evening chores. Will and Bleu lingered over cider at the table while Sylvie and Jolie went out onto the humid porch with Brielle. There they sat in cane chairs, their voices hushed in the humid twilight. Yawning, Jolie climbed onto her mother's lap, her head against her shoulder.

"So, how are you faring in the settlement gardens?" Sylvie asked.

Was Sylvie testing her contentment?

Brielle took out a hand fan and waved it to scatter insects as much as cool her face. "I find the work fulfilling if unending. With so many to feed year round ..."

"You're a huge help," Sylvie said. "But perhaps a change is needed now that the first of the harvest is finished. I've seen you with the settlement children. They follow after you like a hen with chicks."

"Being with the children is where my heart is."

"Extra hands are always needed in the day nursery. We've nineteen children now, six of them *bébés* and more on the way. I've told Will a bigger building must be had, away from the river. Little ones are so tempted by water …"

"The older children are good at helping keep the littlest ones safe."

"True. We've not had a drowning yet though we've come close a time or two." Sylvie folded hands across her expanding waist. "I'll be glad of your help come my confinement, too. I've not long to wait by my reckoning."

"Another month or so," Madeleine said, joining them. "Have you any names in mind?"

"If another girl I may name her after my mother or Will's though sometimes doing so seems a sore reminder of their passing."

"You miss your parents very much, like I do mine."

"Always. Over time the ache lessens but it always lingers. You understand that I'm sure."

"For a long time I tried not to think of what I lost," Brielle told her. "Dwelling on the past made the harshness of the present unbearable. But here, away from the tavern, I'm freer to remember."

"I felt the same when I came here from Williamsburg. So much bustle and fuss there, and so much serenity here. And though we've recently met I'm struck by all that we have in common—and how you seem more sister than friend."

The similarities were striking. Once Sylvie had been without a home, even a house, and husband. Her family had been torn from her. Though she rarely spoke of it, the pensive lines in her face told of her past heartache.

"Someday you'll have your own home, your own family and you'll find that the Almighty fills the emptiness with Himself along with countless other blessings."

Brielle bit her lip lest she confide her stubborn fear of having to leave and return to servitude. That somehow Bleu's redemption of them was flawed and she and Titus weren't free after all. Yet one thing she knew, one truth she held onto—

"God has already shown me great mercy through Bleu."

"My brother has always been quick to show compassion, to understand the plight of others less fortunate."

"Most men would have left us to fend for ourselves without another thought." She nearly shuddered at the memory of Wade Griffiths. "I wish that I could repay your brother in some way. I feel beholden to him though he's assured me I am not."

Understanding shone in Sylvie's eyes. "I felt much the same when Will asked me to marry him. I was a broken, beholden young woman, more girl really, never having been beyond Acadie. He showed me that same mercy though I pushed him away at first."

"There has been no pushing away of Bleu." Brielle smiled a bit sheepishly. "My worry is that I might wake up one morning and he'll be gone."

Sylvie's smile became a sigh. "My brother is like the wind, one never knows when or where it will blow."

Was his shattered past part of his restlessness? Never settling, always seeking?

"He is *extraordinaire*, turning a hand to nearly anything, it seems." Brielle couldn't hide her pride or her pleasure. "Orchardist, farrier, farmer, ferryman. Even a respected guide and interpreter."

"We tease and say he could turn tinker if he chose, able to do so many things well," Sylvie agreed, looking down at Jolie. "He's of great benefit to the settlement and I hope one day he'll stay. I've been holding onto that hope ever since I came here."

"Perhaps," Brielle ventured, "he simply needs a reason to remain."

19

ithin the confines of Will's study adjoining the dining room, Bleu sat near an open window, his whole being pulled to the porch. He could hear the soft hum of Sylvie's and Brielle's voices and wondered what they talked about. His brother-in-law lit a pipe and he did the same, the smoky fragrance of Tidewater tobacco suffusing the warm air. The chamber's paneled walls were a dusky blue, a painting of Acadie's *Baie Française* above the fireless hearth's mantel. It returned him to the four fireplaces lacking mantels beyond the orchard.

"Now is the time to finish my house," Bleu said, exhaling a purl of smoke.

Will stared at him. "Why?"

Bleu chuckled. His brother-in-law was forthright, often carrying conversations on a single syllable. "I am no longer the Resistance fighter of Acadie. I am getting restless ... to remain in one place."

Will's brows rose, his stoicism shifting to surprise. "Sylvie's prayers are finally being answered in that regard then. You ken how I feel about the matter, to say nothing of the children. Does this have to do with the young woman on the porch?"

Leaning forward, Bleu closed the window in answer.

Will's amusement was plain. "So, after all these years, with countless settlement women eyeing you and vying for you, you've settled on someone else entirely."

"Do you believe in coincidence?"

"Nay. Divine instances, rather."

"This is one of them."

Bleu still pondered the events that led him to the *Rose and Crown* with a sort of bafflement. He recounted them now to Will as succinctly as he could. In all his comings and goings, he had never passed that way though he'd crossed paths with hunters and trappers who often did. And he'd happened by on the very Sabbath of the Indian raid. Only Brielle and Titus had stayed standing, another miracle.

"You could have buried the dead, seen the living safely settled, then ridden away," Will remarked.

"That was my first thought. But in the end, it seemed callous to leave a frightened boy and young woman to fend for themselves." Brielle's terrified gaze—her collapse in the dusty road—still wrenched him. "I understand what it's like to have everything torn away from you at once."

Will nodded, his gaze traveling to the closed window again. "You're in love with her."

Sabine had said the same but with far more heat. Remembering, Bleu wanted to forget their fraught exchange. "Be that as it may, *Mademoiselle* Farrow is far removed from a Métis like me."

"How so?"

"She has family in Europe. I keep wondering if she shouldn't take the next ship to England or France instead of staying here on the Rivanna."

"That would be for her to decide, right?"

Bleu shifted in his chair, already seeing her there, bedecked in silks and laces, waited on instead of cast in the role of servant, a world away from the humble life she'd known here.

Will's intent gaze held his for one dissecting moment. "Why not ask her to wed you instead?"

The honest words went to his head like fine brandy. But he wouldn't allow himself to entertain the thought overlong.

"As I told Sylvie, she feels indebted to me which is not the best foundation for a lifelong commitment. I would have … more."

"Once I thought your sister wed me out of desperation because she had nowhere else to go. A ploy of the enemy of our souls, mayhap, to plant doubt, suspicion, and destroy any good the Almighty means to give us."

True. Still … "I would wait awhile. Finish the house. Determine how she feels about being here and moving forward."

"As for the house, all you lack are Crown glass windows, a finished staircase, mantels and paint. And a decent front porch and some furnishings. As for Miss Farrow, you might consider assigning Noir to guard her from the onslaught of suitors sure to ensue."

Will's humor didn't relieve him.

"She is *très beau, oui.*" Bleu expelled another pent-up breath. "On the other hand, perhaps other suitors would help her determine who and what she wants in future."

Yet the very thought set him on edge. He'd rather endure the rigors of returning to Canada than watch any courtship other than their own play out along the Rivanna. The possibility of losing her was excruciating and she wasn't even his. Was that not love?

And the adoration he'd read in her own eyes …

Was that simply because she saw him as her earthly savior?

Brielle rose early, before the settlement roosters crowed, and left Titus asleep in the cottage. Stepping off the porch, she walked through the orchard to Bleu's unfinished house, her hem dew-drenched by the time she reached it. The view drew her. She wanted to see the sunrise and ponder a life spent beholding those mountains and valleys in future. Mornings along the Rivanna when all was silent except for birdsong seemed especially hallowed.

She sat on the bottom step of the partial front porch, a warm wind toying with her carefully pinned cap and the edges of her apron. Bending her head, she breathed a prayer into the stillness, hoping to quell the unrest inside her. A short prayer, childlike in its simplicity, but encompassing so many of her unspoken womanly yearnings.

Heavenly Father, help me savor the goodness of the present rather than fret about the unknown future. Amen.

She opened her eyes, the sunrise spreading across the horizon like melted butter. Her stomach growled in response. She must be hungry if the sun resembled an egg and she craved toast and tea.

Would Bleu be at breakfast?

The thought nearly sent her down the hill but in truth it was too early to break one's fast nor had the bell rung summoning the settlement to the kitchen house. After breakfast she would spend her hours in the day nursery next to the still-room, tending to other's children when what she wanted was a houseful of her own.

As she thought it, a noise in the orchard turned her head. Several Acadians carrying tools cleared the rows of apple trees and began climbing the hill. Before she could leap from her perch into the grass and disappear, she spied Bleu coming behind the other men, most of them settlement carpenters, a ladder across one sturdy shoulder. Her desire to disappear fled.

When he saw her, he set his burden down, stopping just shy of the steps. His eyes were smiling. "*Bonjour, Mademoiselle Farrow.*"

When he said it he seemed to speak with the respect granted royalty. It left her flushed and joyous all at once. "I had to come up the hill again to see the sunrise."

"Perhaps one day we'll watch it together," he told her before he hefted the ladder again and resumed walking around the side of the house.

"You're finishing your work here?" she called after him.

He looked over his shoulder. "Now is the time, *oui*. I should have finished long ago."

Elated, she nearly skipped down the hill when the breakfast bell sounded only he caught up with her on the riverside path, the men following, obviously intent on a hearty meal before a day's work.

"And what did you make of the sunrise?" he asked.

"As splendid as the sunset."

"Should I build a grander *porche* with posts so we can better take it in?"

She didn't miss the *we* nor would she let herself dwell on its implications—or the lack of them. A slip of the tongue? Or a heartfelt hope?

"What will you name it?" she asked him.

"The house?"

"Sylvie named Orchard Rest. Surely you can think of something."

His smile held mischief. "Perhaps that task is best left to you."

Her mind went blank at the delightful prospect.

"There's to be a *fête*, did Sylvie tell you?"

"Nay—*non*." Her head nearly spun as she swerved between Anglais and Français. "What sort of *fête*?"

"Dancing. Feasting. Much music and merriment."

A qualm beset her that she'd be on the outside again. Not Acadian. Not even a Virginian. "I've quite forgotten how to dance though I had a dancing master long ago in Philadelphia."

He gave her another long look. "Then meet me in the orchard at dusk."

Their eyes locked, his in warm invitation, hers clouded with uncertainty though a tingling anticipation coursed through her.

Dusk couldn't come soon enough.

Brielle arrived in the orchard before Bleu. She could still hear hammering up the hill. Was he still at work? She'd seen him only briefly at supper when he'd come in late to the kitchen house once she'd finished her meal and rose from the table. She and Titus took turns eating at Orchard Rest and then with the settlement though Sabine's presence continued to unsettle her. But lately the fiery-haired Acadian who spent her days in the stillroom hadn't sought her out like at first.

She looked down, smoothing her linen petticoat and snatching at a stray string. Sylvie had been sewing a pretty gown for her and the delight and secretiveness with which she'd gone about her task delighted Brielle in turn. The promised garment would be finished by the *fête* next Saturday. She'd dress the part, at least, and hope she could manage the dancing.

Just when she thought he might have forgotten to meet her, she looked up to see Bleu coming through the apple trees, so handsome even in simple clothes that she framed the moment in her head and heart. As he walked he rolled down his linen sleeves and buttoned them, a skim of sawdust on his breeches and boots. Coatless and hatless, he hardly seemed the dancing master but something told her he was no novice.

"I am unfit for dancing, *Mademoiselle* Farrow," he called out. "But I've looked forward to this all day."

"As have I." Her heart picked up like they'd already begun a jig. "If you dance like you ride, *Monsieur Galant*, I've no cause to complain."

He stood in front of her and gave a small, gallant bow.

She nodded as a dim, dusty recollection caused her to curtsy. Slowly, he took four steps to the right then faced her before taking four steps to the left and returning to his original position. She did the same, imitating him, taking his outstretched right hand. His callused touch was both rousing and reassuring as she followed his lead, moving in a small circle before switching to their left hands and repeating the steps.

Next they joined hands and circled each other. *Allemande*, he'd said. Or was it *poussette*? They went deeper into the orchard, moving around young apple scions as if they were imaginary couples, twirling in the grass to the tune of the rising wind as twilight hemmed them in.

"You *do* dance as well as you ride," she said, trying to catch her breath.

He came to a stop but he didn't let go of her hand. He was hardly winded. Oh, how he held her heart still. The summer sun had darkened his skin, making his eyes more fiercely blue, his queued hair a glossy blue-black. He was so handsome it hurt, causing a flare of anguish inside her.

Raising her hand and holding her gaze, he brushed his lips against her sun-browned fingers. "You don't belong in an orchard but a ballroom."

"I prefer an orchard."

"Though you say you've forgotten how to dance you have not. It's in your blood, your lineage." He let go of her hand. "*Une princesse du sang*."

She smiled at his teasing. "A princess of the blood I am not."

"And I am no prince but a dusty, disheveled carpenter, at least today." He looked toward the river. "What I need is a bath."

She almost sighed, wishing she could join him for that, too. "I'll be counting the hours till the *fête*. Shall I save a dance for you?"

"*Oui.*" He turned back to her, expression intent. "More than one."

20

$\mathcal{B}$ rielle nearly held her breath when Sylvie led her into an upstairs bedchamber at Orchard Rest to show her the altered gown. Of Lyonnais silk, the pale-yellow fabric with its vivid patterned fruits and flowers shimmered in the afternoon's fading light where it lay across the bed. Exquisite blonde lace overlay the bodice and sleeve ruffles. The petticoat was also trimmed in lace, the open skirt drawn up by hidden linen tapes. Shoes of a matching color waited on the floor with ribbon closures. Sylvie had even thought of a hand fan, its painted edges lace trimmed.

"Every dress tells a story," Sylvie told her, examining the hem with a seamstress's eye. "Long ago, Bleu returned home in a snowstorm with this fabric in his haversack. Though we didn't know it then, that was to be our last Christmas in Acadie. I carried the finished dress with me when the British expelled us as it was my most treasured possession. But I haven't worn it since my wedding day. And it's much too lovely to be shut away."

Brielle touched a sleeve ruffle. "It's the loveliest gown I've ever seen."

"I couldn't find anything finer in Williamsburg on our last trip, so I altered it to fit you."

Brielle touched the colorful petticoat then tried on the shoes. Oddly they fit. Beside them were clocked silk stockings and a pair of garters. "You've thought of everything."

"I've some jewelry to borrow if you like," Sylvie said, clearly pleased. "Pearls from the Galants of long ago."

Brielle thought of *Maman's* jewelry box and the keepsakes she'd never worn as her daughter. Perfect for a French ball, perhaps, but not a colonial American dance on a remote river few had heard of. Once again, she wondered why Sylvie treated her more like family, hardly a stranger or even one of the settlement women. Did Bleu have something to do with that?

The next hour was a flurry of bathing and dressing and attempting a coiffure fit for a *fête*, curling tongs and all. The finishing touch was the Galant pearls about her neck. Standing before a looking glass, Brielle felt she was someone else entirely. The gown's history involving Bleu made it even more meaningful.

Joining hands, Amélie, Jolie, and Madeleine danced around her skirts with childish praise. "*Si belle, si élégante!*"

Bleu waited downstairs, they told her. Turning away from the looking glass, Brielle left the bedchamber and started her descent in the new shoes, lace fan dangling from a lemon-yellow ribbon encircling her wrist. Sylvie kept the girls upstairs, putting finishing touches on their own party dresses.

Bleu stood at the bottom step. When she paused on the landing his eyes went wide. Was he remembering the snowstorm of long ago? The long journey the exquisite silk had taken, first with him and then his sister? The joy she'd had when he'd given it to her? For once he seemed at a loss for words, but his gaze never wavered as she reached the last step.

"I remember that silk …" he murmured.

"Too lovely to be shut away, Sylvie said."

He reached out and touched a sleeve ruffle. "And now I'm thinking it wasn't meant for my sister but you."

She smiled at the fanciful thought, that long ago he had chosen the fabric for her instead, a woman he had yet to meet. Perhaps the gown was meant to be passed down in the family, from one wedding to the next.

The tender moment was undone by the noisy tumult of his nieces and nephews as Will and Sylvie led their brood out the front door and down the hill, each bedecked in their best, while Bleu followed behind with Brielle, his hand at her elbow. Titus was already at the river with numerous other children, dressed in the shirt and breeches she'd made him.

The sound of fiddle music and the scent of roasting meat permeated the humid late June air. In the flickering, dramatic light of the cressets—burning iron baskets hanging from poles—Brielle did a quick count of nearly one hundred Acadians. What a picture the women made in their colorful dresses adorned with a rainbow of ribbons and streamers. The custom of Acadie? And a great many wooden shoes. *Sabots*, Sylvie said. The men dressed much like Bleu in finely tailored shirts and dark breeches, a few in waistcoats.

Bleu left her side to speak with some of the men while Brielle kept close to Sylvie. Dressed in green brocade, her advancing pregnancy apparent, she was quick to sit yet greeted everyone graciously, introducing Brielle to those she didn't know. Benches lined the south riverbank, and the kitchen house doors stood open. As the *porc* was raised from the pit, women set out vegetables and bread of all kinds as well as ale and cider.

"First the feasting, then the dancing," Sylvie told her as a line formed.

Brielle removed her fan from the ribbon at her wrist and opened it. "Do you often have these gatherings?"

"Once a month, usually, aside from weddings and christenings and such. It's been our tradition since the settlement's founding, a rest from our labors and a celebration of God's bounty foremost."

Sabine Broussard was first in line, reminding Brielle of Bleu's refusal to return her to Acadie. At the sound of his voice, Sabine looked back at them, unsmiling. Uncomfortable, Brielle pivoted toward Bleu who now stood so close she caught the Castile soap scent of him.

His gaze lowered to her throat. "You're wearing the Galant pearls."

She fingered the necklace, warm against her skin. "Sylvie is as bighearted as you are."

"Bighearted? My sister just evicted me from her house."

"What?"

"I'm now in mine, rough as it is. But the staircase is nearly done." His voice held an enthusiasm she'd not heard before, even regret. "It doesn't curve quite like yours in Philadelphia nor is there an angel in an alcove—"

She put a finger to his lips to shush him. "There needn't be."

He smiled and her hand fell away. Their close rapport was garnering attention and not only Sabine's. Suddenly shamefaced, Brielle moved forward in line, turning away from him.

Her attention swung to desserts on a far table. "*Tarte à la rhubarbe*? And *gâteau à la mélasse*?"

"You make me want to finish my kitchen," he said behind her.

Suddenly sweets were the furthest thing from her mind. She was all too aware of him—and Sabine—and the notice being paid her in her Lyonnais silk gown. Sabine left the kitchen house, her head held high like an Acadian queen while Brielle suddenly felt an imposter, a tavern maid, trying to fit in and find her place.

If Virginians were said to be the finest dancers among His Majesty's colonials, surely the Acadians weren't far behind them. Bleu's lesson in the orchard helped smooth Brielle's steps and nerves. Once supper had settled, he claimed her for the first dance, a lively reel, and though she didn't step it perfectly she learned quickly and didn't repeat her mistakes.

Bleu partnered with Sylvie next and then Sabine while Brielle danced with several men she didn't know as the clock ticked toward midnight. Winded and exhilarated, she wanted nothing more than to be away from the melee and alone with Bleu. But he seemed to have forgotten about her, talking and laughing with his fellow Acadians when he wasn't dancing, sometimes disappearing altogether. When Sabine vanished, too, Brielle felt a qualm.

What was the gist of their relationship?

Titus sidled up to her and gave a charming little bow. "You look pretty tonight, not all worn out like you did at the tavern."

Amused by his honesty, she sat down on a bench facing the river, patting the seat beside her. "How good it is to be worn out from a *fête* instead."

He nodded as he turned his back on the swirl of dancers. "I just want this frolic to be over so I can return to the river. Bleu's going to take me fishing again tomorrow after I help him put up shelves in his kitchen."

Ah, the kitchen, in need of her own special rhubarb tart. She felt a bone-deep contentment thinking of the clean, whitewashed space, followed by an ache that it might someday belong to someone else instead.

"Look at this hook and lure he made." He dug into his pocket then held it aloft in the flickering light of the cressets. "He took one of Mrs. Blackburn's sewing needles and bent it to shape, then carved this lure of willow and stained it in the dying shed. Now it only needs a feather to finish."

Brielle studied it, impressed. "You're becoming quite the fisherman. I even heard you're helping build a stone weir upriver."

"I'm making a reed weir for streams, too, but first Bleu taught me to swim."

Had he?

Titus eyed her curiously. "Can you swim?"

"I cannot but perhaps Bleu can teach me, too." The idea of being reduced to smallclothes in the middle of the river suddenly held great appeal. "I've not even ferried across the Rivanna yet."

"I have." His small chest swelled with pride. "Jean-Marc, the ferryman, said he might take me on as his right hand."

Suddenly Titus seemed far older than his eight years. So many interests and plans he had while she bounced from one task to the next, never sure of herself or what she did, including the next step.

"I'm glad you're happy here and of help." She draped an arm about his shoulders and hugged him close. "Our old life over-mountain seems like it never was."

They sat in the shadows in companionable quiet as the fiddle music showed signs of waning, a few people departing as the full moon rose in a cloudless sky.

Coming up behind them unawares, Bleu took a seat on the bench, Titus between them. "Ready to return to the cottage?"

Brielle met Bleu's eyes briefly, not minding a whit that Titus was already on his feet, his mind clearly on the morrow and a good night's sleep. She got to her feet as Bleu, without a lantern, simply led them on the path he'd walked so many times before.

When they reached the cottage, they said goodnight. Titus disappeared inside, and she followed only to reappear on the porch and watch Bleu climb the hill to his house. Was he sleeping upstairs there? Somehow that seemed to suggest his staying in Virginia, assuaging her unsettled heart. Only his handsome house deserved a name.

What would it be?

21

*L*ate July brought a lushness to the settlement's gardens that defied description. In the orchard, ripe peaches and cherries hung heavy on the trees while apples of all varieties promised a bountiful autumn harvest. Albemarle Pippins and Fameuses were Sylvie's pride. Already the settlement was abuzz, anticipating the abundant cider to come. If the Acadians had a favorite season, it had to be autumn.

Would Bleu still be here then?

Soon after the *fête* came a wedding. The riverside chapel nearly burst with Acadians as the couple tied the knot, turning Brielle's thoughts to her own heart. But Bleu seemed to have taken another step back. Perhaps it was because he was busy in the fields now, away from the heart of the settlement. The tobacco harvest had begun, every hand needed. Even Will had set aside his surveying for the time being.

"Should I be in the fields?" Brielle asked Sylvie, never wanting to shirk work.

"You're most needed here in the nursery, especially with so many in the fields." Sylvie smiled her reassurance as children gathered around them, a flaxen-haired baby in Brielle's lap, a fat fist in his mouth. "You've also helped fill the hole Henrietta left when she moved with her brother, Nolan, and his Acadian wife last winter."

"Your adopted children, the two orphans? Bleu mentioned how much you miss them."

"They lived on the Rivanna since the settlement's founding. But then Nolan came of age and apprenticed to an Alexandria silversmith Will knows. They visit when they can—and we go visit them in turn."

"I've heard of Alexandria. I'd like to see another town besides Philadelphia though I have no desire to live in a place teeming with people," Brielle told her. "The Rivanna River seems idyllic. I don't want to be anywhere else on earth."

"I felt the same when I left Williamsburg. I'd been working in a bookbindery before becoming a French tutor and seamstress at the Governor's Palace. Once I saw Orchard Rest I never wanted to leave it though life here, like everywhere, has its flaws."

Flaws? So far she'd found none or was her every perception colored by Bleu?

"I remember the stench of Philadelphia and the reek of tar and fish and saltwater." Brielle wiped the baby's damp chin with her apron hem. "And all the refuse in narrow alleys and the huge market on High Street. Summers were stifling and winters harsh with the Atlantic winds."

"Virginia's heat and insects drive me half mad sometimes and the dreary damp in winter hurts my bones, but spring and fall are an ongoing pleasure and I'd rather raise a family here than anywhere else. Every season has its own particular beauty."

"I hope to experience them all."

"Have you ever considered traveling to meet your relatives?"

Brielle looked at her. Had she been talking to Bleu?

"I've no funds to do so … and less courage. My father's family I know little about other than they once resided in the West Midlands. My French relations are also strangers." Truly, to risk an ocean and the unknown, given her kinfolk might reject her outright or think her an imposter, seemed especially rash. "I'm content right here."

Content paled with what she felt. Despite any uncertainty about the future, she finally had her freedom yet far more. How was it possible to describe her certainty she'd come home? Come home to both a person and a place, even if that person didn't realize it yet?

Her heart felt so full it might burst. "I want to be of help in any way I can to express my gratitude."

"I'll welcome your help once the baby arrives," Sylvie looked to her own waist, or the lack of one. "And I'm wondering if these aren't twins as I'm so *énorme*. After several children, I am somewhat expert, though childbirth is fraught with uncertainty every time."

"Are there twins in your family?"

"*Oui,* on my mother's side." Her delight darkened. "But our kin were scattered clear to the Caribbean after the expulsion. Many, we believe, have perished."

"Bleu spoke of your brothers, Pascal and Lucien, and wanting to know what happened to them." Holding the drowsy infant close, Brielle said, "Your family history is even sadder than my own."

All the more reason to marry and continue the lineage that had been lost.

The next day, Brielle returned to the cottage after another midday meal at the kitchen house without Bleu. Wistful, she went to a rear window and studied the shade trees atop the hill that ringed the house where loud hammering drove home her curiosity. Time seemed chafingly slow in his absence, but she wouldn't run up the hill and interrupt his work. Simply wanting to see him wouldn't do.

Instead she opened a cupboard and took out her jewelry box. Inlaid with mother-of-pearl, its fleur-de-lis motif had beautiful chasing on the sides and a miniature portrait of her mother on the lid. *Maman*—Josseline Vérany—had been painted as a young woman prior to her marriage. She was unmistakably her mother's daughter though she only shared her father's green eyes. Perhaps she would see more of her English ancestry in her children's faces someday.

She opened the lid to reveal a gold ring, too large for her finger, and a *rivière* necklace with cross pendant. When her mother had fled France, she'd taken little with her except the box and its contents. And it had taken pride of place in *Maman's* bedchamber, saved for Brielle when she came of age.

She'd shown no one these possessions, a bit fearful that she, a tavern maid, might be accused of theft. Even handling them brought a poignancy she couldn't put into words. So, she'd secreted it, storing it away, her one heirloom. Her mother had given it to her on her sixteenth birthday right before she'd fallen ill. Her soft words, spoken in the height of fever, seemed embroidered on Brielle's spirit.

This is your heritage. All I have left to give you. Once I was of a grand, noble family but I have learned one's happiness doesn't depend on one's fortune. I have been rich indeed to have loved both your father and you. I can ask for nothing more in this life if I am to leave and be with my Father in heaven.

Afterwards, Brielle had written them down and placed them inside the box. The scrap of paper was old and worn from repeated perusing, the ink faded. But it still carried the same poignancy and left her eyes smarting.

There had been times in lean years when she was so hungry and worn she could have sold her heirlooms for food and other comforts. But being hungry and having a treasure was worth far more than being full and bereft.

22

*B*leu stood back and surveyed the staircase in the central hall. Made of oak, it bespoke strength and longevity, able to endure a century or more. A straight flight, it bore narrow steps that he hoped weren't too steep. The fleur-de-lis engraved on the newel post at the stairs' bottom made him wonder if Brielle would notice. He'd had it crafted in the settlement's carpentry with her in mind.

"Last window is finally in!" Will's satisfied bellow carried from the second floor. "Wise to choose Crown glass instead of cylinder or bullseye. Far less distortion though one might think you were a high and mighty Burgess rather than a *truchement*."

"*Truchement?*" Bleu chuckled as Will descended the steps with his oldest sons. "I haven't heard that old French Acadian word for some time."

"I've always preferred it to interpreter or guide or runner."

"And now I am a poorer *truchement* having purchased the finest English glass to be had."

Will gestured to the front door newly hung on dovetail hinges. "The early apples—*Summer Rambour*—are being pressed down by the river. Shall we celebrate and have cider?"

"You've earned it." Bleu drew the front door shut and took another look at the gleaming windows.

Will started down the hill ahead of him, Corbin and Talbot by his side. Bleu followed, eyes on the barely visible cottage at the foot of the hill. Was Brielle there? Late afternoons often found her in Orchard Rest's kitchen or garden, helping Sylvie now that it was near her time. He saw her seldom since he often ate from a knapsack in the fields or while working on his house. There was no denying he missed her. Missed her ready smile and bubbling laugh. The endearing way she'd look at him, a light in her eyes.

He walked through the orchard, some trees so heavily laden their branches nearly touched the ground. As they neared the river a pink-cheeked Madeleine appeared, her expression indecipherable.

"Papa, 'tis time! Eve—the midwife—is with *Maman*. She needs your prayers but doesn't want you at the house till all is said and done."

Will stopped walking, looking at his oldest daughter with concern. "Tell her I'll pray, aye, and to send for me at any time. We'll be down by the river at the cider-making."

Madeleine nodded, darting a shy look at Bleu as if he shouldn't be privy to such womanly things. Bleu glanced at Will, amazed by his response. If this was Brielle he wouldn't continue calmly to the river … but it was what it was. And William Blackburn *was* a seasoned father of six, soon to be seven.

"Shall we place wagers?" Will jested, clamping a firm hand on his sons' shoulders as they walked on either side of him. "Boy or girl?"

"Boy," Talbot returned with a grin.

"Girl," Corbin said with confidence.

"The last, our Jolie, was born within a few hours," Will reminded them, "so we might not have long to wait."

They reached the Rivanna where the tang of crushed apples mingled with the clean scent of river water. Acadians of all ages gathered round a large oaken press, feeding fruit to the mill. Endless baskets of picked apples waited, not the rich, spicy cider apples of the later harvest but the sweet, refreshing blend of the first.

Bleu stood by a long trough where apple juice ran in rivulets to an open tub. Empty barrels stood by to store the finished cider. It seemed he'd taken a step back to the boy he'd been in Acadie, breathing in the intoxicating perfume of ripe fruit, carrying the burlap bags of apple mash to feed the livestock, his reward a full cup of the golden juice that wasn't bound for the cellar.

He took a drink from the first press, wanting to share the moment with Brielle but contenting himself with the fact her time was far better spent uphill. His own prayer for Sylvie was fervent if silent. Will, too, looked preoccupied, his outward calm for the benefit of his young sons who needn't worry about their beloved mother, Bleu guessed.

To be a father …

He couldn't imagine it, hadn't let himself imagine it before this. But having met Brielle his thoughts raced ahead to their wedding day. The birth of their firstborn. More children after that. Generation upon generation on this very ground. But before he told her his feelings, he needed to settle another matter first.

What if she was meant for more?

"Bleu." Sabine's voice returned him to the present.

He turned and schooled his reaction at the intrusion. His old friend didn't deserve his disdain simply because she reminded him of a lost world—or that she wasn't Brielle. He greeted her, well aware everything had been taken from her, too.

She reached for an apple yet to be mashed and bit into it, chewing and swallowing before she said, "Cidermaking turns my thoughts to winter and making the most of traveling before the snow sets in."

He nodded, understanding that, too. Till now, his roaming life had hinged on the seasons. "Are you willing to take my offer of a trustworthy guide?"

"Tell me more about him."

"John Riel is Métis—country-born with an English father."

"*Les métis anglais.*"

"Quiet. Reliable. A master of the woods. Last I heard he's wanting to return to Canada and Hudson's Bay for trading but is near Staunton at present."

"Not far, then."

"I could send word. Arrange a meeting."

Her smile held mischief. "Only if you're sure you don't want to return, too."

"I want to return to the Acadie of old which is no more." He put the matter to rest once and for all. "But I can certainly help you get there if you so choose."

Standing at the foot of the bed mounded with pillows and fresh linens, Brielle watched as the settlement midwife bathed Sylvie's face with a sponge. She was alarmingly flushed, her jaw set to keep from crying out as one hour turned into two.

Embarrassment burned through Brielle along with astonishment. That two people coming together could create a child ... and then *this*. Dying she knew to be distressing. She had witnessed her parents succumb, the ordeal a scar on her tender conscience. Giving birth, this raw, brazen coming into the world, was just as harrowing, too.

She prayed as she tried to assist, ruing the hot August day. Sylvie's hair hung in damp wisps about her pinked face, her shift clinging to her. Between pangs she smiled and even laughed a time or two but as the pain worsened, anticipation hung thick in the room, joy pushed to a shadowed corner.

Needing to fetch more water, Brielle went downstairs. The chicken she'd roasted waited on the kitchen's spit, herbed vegetables in a pot alongside it, loaves of bread on the trestle table beside freshly churned, salted butter. Later, once the ordeal was done, a famished Sylvie would have a small feast.

Taking hold of a pail, Brielle went out the back door to the well. Lowering the rope, she tried to draw a deep breath as the hot, windless day pressed her on all sides, a fly bedeviling her. As she wound the full pail to the top a baby's cry rent the air, a great, gasping howl that surely signaled health. Through the second floor's open windows she heard the midwife's voice before Sylvie's—both of them jubilant. Relieved.

Brielle hastened back into the house, toting the pail carefully so not to spill a drop. At the bedchamber's entrance she saw Sylvie cradling an infant that had miraculously quieted as if lulled by his mother's loving voice. Not twins, after all. But all was well, she sensed, even before the midwife plunged the newborn into a near basin of water only to set the baby howling again.

Exhausted but elated, Sylvie lay back against the bank of pillows. "A robust boy, thank heavens."

Will and the children soon came uphill to meet the new addition. Amid the fanfare and fuss, Sylvie said to Brielle, "Why don't you go tell my brother our glad news and have some cider?"

Brielle fairly ran from Orchard Rest to the riverbank. She was thirsty, having forgotten to drink a drop during the delivery. Though all seemed well, a smidgen of concern remained. Would Sylvie recover? She'd looked terribly worn at the last …

A prayer on her lips, she took in the river, the cidermaking finished, a small cask remaining on the bank. A wagon hauled the rest toward the settlement's cellars, most of the Acadians with it. A lone woman—Sabine—tarried, but to her relief, hurried after the cider wagon when she saw Brielle, leaving Bleu alone.

Unaware of her approach, he stood, back to her, looking across the water with its eternal rush. She wondered his private thoughts as the sun began its fiery descent toward the mountains.

"*Joyeux* tidings," she said a bit breathlessly as she came to stand beside him. "Your sister is well and you have another nephew."

He smiled, his teeth a flash of white. "His name?"

She felt a trill of delight delivering the news. "Bleu Blackburn."

Surprise held them still for a few hallowed moments.

"I've never been here at such a time," he said, eyes glinting.

"I've never witnessed such a miracle."

"A miracle, *oui*. Do you want *enfants* of your own?"

"Ask me another day," she half jested.

He darted an amused glance at her. "Not for the faint of heart, *ma chère*?"

She warmed to the endearment. "Today reminded me that even beautiful things can be hard."

"Much of life is like that." He went to the cask to refill his pewter cup and handed it to her.

"Thank you." Parched, she drank it quickly. "Refreshing. Sweet yet a bit tart."

He took the cup back and set it on the bank as the settlement's bell sounded. "Should we tarry here or have supper?"

"Do you want to see your sister?"

"I'll see her—and my namesake—in time."

Time. She'd seen Bleu so little of late. What would a few more minutes matter? Turning away discreetly, she bent to remove her shoes and stockings.

The river rippled a deep blue-grey. She waded up to her ankles, her petticoats held aloft. He started upriver, barefoot, then turned back and held out his hand to her, an invitation in his eyes.

"Follow me?" he asked.

"Anywhere," she answered with a half-smile, clasping his callused hand.

He led her to a cove where willow trees clustered, their long graceful branches trailing in the shallows. A dove cooed, a bittersweet sound she'd always loved. When she looked uphill from here she had a clear view of his house.

"Anywhere?" He faced her, their fingers still entwined. "Even to France?"

His gaze was intent, not teasing, and she felt a little start. He was speaking of faraway France when what she wanted was for him to kiss her. He was so near her bare feet fit between his. If he would only take her in his arms ...

"*Alors dis moi,*" she finally said. *So, tell me.*

He reached out and brushed her cheek with the back of his fingers. "To the Loire Valley and Charles Vérany, *comte de Sancerre.*"

"My grandfather?" Her words held fear and fascination. "Why?"

"Why not?" he replied gently.

She was the first to look away lest he read the answer in her eyes.

I have no desire to go to France when I simply want to stay right here with you.

"I've considered it for some time." He spoke slowly as if he was not wanting to overwhelm her. "We could sail from York Town. The passage takes four to eight weeks depending on conditions. We would stay as little or as long as you like. Long enough to meet your grandfather and see where your mother came from.

The Loire Valley is said to be very beautiful. Very different from here."

She looked back at him. "You've given this much thought."

"Nothing is as important as family. It took me losing mine, save Sylvie, to realize that fact."

"But what if the *comte de Sancerre* doesn't want to be met?"

"A risk we have to take." He smiled, turning her heart over again. "But who could refuse you?"

Philadelphia's shimmering harbor returned in a frightening rush, ships' masts dense as a forest. "I've never been on board a ship, never crossed anything but a river. Hardly an ocean."

"Nor have I."

"You weren't one of the Acadians expelled by boat."

"I eluded the English by going further inland with the Mi'qmak instead. Then, when I realized the British had come to stay and fighting further was useless, I traveled south on foot and horseback to the colonies."

"I'm not sure I can weather an ocean voyage." She swallowed, terrified at the thought. "Ships sink—there are storms—seasickness. Drownings. Pirates and enemy warships."

"We'll weather it together."

"But I have not said *oui*."

Again, that amused glint in his eyes. "You have not said *non* either." He placed his hands on her shoulders. "If it helps, there's a young woman from the settlement—Nadine Durand—who has wanted to see family in France for some time."

"She would be my traveling companion, you mean. When I can't be with you."

"It benefits you both. I am simply your escort."

Simply. There was nothing simple about this. She felt dizzy even considering such an impromptu plan. "But I have no funds."

"I have enough for us all, even Mademoiselle Durand, though Will has arranged to pay her way there and back, if she chooses."

Such benevolence continued to be a marvel to her after all the grasping, greedy men at the *Rose and Crown*. "And once again, if we do go, I am indebted to you."

"*Non*, Brielle. I owe you."

Without further explanation, he began leading her back down the riverbank to where their discarded shoes and stockings waited, his firm hand holding hers once again as the shallow water frothed around their bare legs.

"Time to meet my namesake," he said, looking toward Orchard Rest.

"And have supper," she reminded him though she doubted she'd eat a bite after what he'd just told her.

23

he next Sabbath, Bleu looked at Brielle across Orchard Rest's table as supper ended and the children excused themselves to do their evening chores. His namesake rested in a basket near Sylvie, fast asleep through the meal but now beginning to fuss.

Brielle set her fork aside and he saw she'd not finished her blackberry tart. She gave him a half-smile, his co-conspirator for the moment. Was she nervous about making their announcement?

Now, in the sudden silence, they'd learn his family's reaction to their news.

Clearing her throat, Brielle said, "Though I'm perfectly happy here, I've decided to accept Bleu's offer to go to France. Having Nadine Durand with us makes the decision easier."

The sudden silence was blessedly brief.

"Our prayers go with you, then." Sylvie reached for the baby, bringing him to her shoulder. If she had any qualms she didn't show it. "In fact, I haven't stopped praying about this since Bleu broached the subject."

Will leaned back in his chair at the head of the table. "I support you fully though I'll warn you the journey, even in the best of conditions, won't be easy but arduous."

"We know the passage will likely be rough." A dozen different scenarios played through Bleu's thoughts all over again. "None of us have been to France and the language is not my French-Acadian patois. I've seen Quebec and Boston and other large cities but Nantes and Paris are another world entirely."

Their eyes met again, hers tender and trusting. Was that trust misplaced? Would she ever regard him with anything other than tenderness? If so, he couldn't bear it. He wanted nothing to hinder this bold and undeniably hazardous plan.

"Aside from the dangers of sea travel, my French family might not want to meet me." Brielle looked from Sylvie to Will. "I have dusty memories of my mother telling me how the *comte* forbade her to marry my father so this may not be the happy reunion I wish for, if he still lives."

A complicated journey, even a courageous one. His chest suddenly felt like a clenched fist. He didn't want to disappoint her or have her hurt. He wanted this to be a homecoming, a door to a future she was denied when her parents died and she was sent into servitude.

"At least you'll soon rest in the fact you tried to reunite with your family, no matter what awaits," Sylvie said. "The Loire Valley isn't called *the garden of France* for naught."

"Do you have anything that might show you are one of the *comte's* kin?" Will asked, as practical as Sylvie was positive.

She nodded. "A small jewelry box *Maman* gave me, with her portrait on the lid. Only two pieces of jewelry remain but I'll take that with me, a sort of introduction, if you will."

Bleu was convinced beauty alone would open doors for Brielle. "I imagine you look enough like her there will be no doubt."

Will took another drink of cider. "I'll secure passage on the best brig with the most competent ship's master I can find. If you go as soon as possible, ahead of hurricane season, fair weather should be in your favor."

"And we'll be here waiting to welcome you home." Sylvie kissed the baby's forehead. "Only this one might be walking by then."

"I regret that," Bleu said. "But I've regretted being away since your firstborn."

A telling titter went round the table. His roaming wouldn't be curtailed till his own children came, Will had once said, if then.

"So, we are going." Again, Brielle's eyes sought Bleu's before returning to her unfinished dessert. "The sooner our passage can be arranged the better."

Lest I change my mind. Bleu guessed her unspoken thoughts.

There seemed a new melancholy about her that eclipsed the joy of living she'd had since she'd walked away from the tavern. Or was she already missing Titus?

"*Tu es sûr*, Bleu?" Sylvie asked, no doubt remembering what he'd said to her upon introducing her to Brielle.

This is my future bride though she may not realize it yet.

He met his sister's eyes.

I spoke too hastily and let my heart rule my head.

Ever since that introduction he'd begun to rein himself in as his vision for Brielle's future widened beyond being Gabrielle Galant to the wife of a *duc* or *marquess* or *comte*, a member of the French nobility from which she'd come. He was willing to set aside his own desires for her best. God's best. Perhaps one day, an ocean apart, full of years and memories, they would still think of each other with affection despite their distance and change in direction.

He held his sister's searching gaze with a stoicism he was far from feeling. "*C'est fait.*"

It is done.

Suddenly everything in the settlement seemed cast in shades of grey. Or was it only her change of mood? Brielle walked from the settlement's nursery at the end of day, when all the children had left with their mothers, and craved the peace of the chapel. The recent wedding that had been held there seared her memory. Though she didn't know the couple well she envied them their newfound happiness.

Entering the empty building, she took a seat on a back pew. Deep gold light streamed through arched windows, reminding her of Philadelphia's stained glass. Sitting there sedately, she inwardly waged a war between delight and dread. Delight to be taking a trip with Bleu. Dread at being tossed like a cork upon the ocean. Fear of what awaited her once they made landfall—*if* they did. With Bleu by her side she'd double the wonders of experiencing France. And be better able to bear the brunt of her grandfather's rejection if it came to that.

A scrap of Psalm came to mind unbidden.

Thou rulest the raging of the sea: when the waves thereof arise, thou stillest them.

The sudden creak of a door turned her head. She looked over her shoulder to see Sabine Broussard enter—like a fox in a henhouse. An unkind comparison, perhaps. Still, Brielle felt an urge to flee.

Sabine came to a stop at the end of the pew where she sat. "I hear you're leaving."

Who had told her? Word traveled fast in the settlement, both good and bad. "Tomorrow we travel to York Town."

"And Bleu will escort you, something he refused to do for me." A resigned sort of bitterness threaded her tone. "Acadie is closer yet he chooses to go a far greater distance instead."

"I cannot answer for Bleu," Brielle told her quietly, wishing he were here to speak for himself.

"Bleu is neither easily swayed nor led. No doubt this journey to France is his idea." She smoothed a ribbon on her skirt. "Nadine's need makes it more convenient for all concerned."

"The opportunity might not come again." Brielle struck a conciliatory tone. "I've prayed about it and trust all will be well."

"You have family in France, so I've heard. Important people, even aristocratic." Sabine seemed to regard her with less hauteur than before. "Given that, you don't belong here. Perhaps Bleu has finally realized it, too. Though you are willing to work and live amongst us you are and forever will be an outsider. The Rivanna settlement seems beneath you."

Brielle looked to her unladylike hands. "Any hard, honest work well done is honorable no matter one's station."

"All that is behind you now." Sabine eyed her shrewdly. "Take care in future and hide your calluses with gloves. Never speak of your former life and what you were reduced to. The French won't care for your colonial ways, especially since they've just lost a terrible war to England, their arch-enemy."

Brielle went still. In the tumult of the past few months she'd only considered France's defeat in a hazy, secondhand way. Perhaps this was not the time to be crossing an ocean in light of that though she knew Bleu had considered it, surely, as their plans moved forward, inch by foolhardy inch. Is that how Sabine saw it?

"Nor will they welcome a Métis who they will no doubt look upon as *sauvage*."

Brielle nearly flinched. Their conversation was circling, continually coming back to Bleu. Did Sabine's jealousy drive her to say such things? If so, she refused to hold it against her. She didn't want to leave the settlement with a bad feeling or any sort of festering confrontation in her mind.

"I need to return to packing," Brielle said, rising from the pew.

Sabine gave her another long look. "Then I wish you well on your journey and hope you find France to be where you belong."

And so the long journey to coastal York Town began, Virginia's foremost seaport. Their sleek, two-masted ship with its ten cannon and thirty crew was called *Courageux*. Fitting, even ironic. Feeling less than courageous, Brielle watched their baggage being brought aboard, her thoughts not on their looming departure but their farewells on the Rivanna River. Emotional, heartfelt farewells that left her second guessing their decision to go.

Bleu had cradled his newborn nephew a final time, unwilling to even give him up when he began to howl. Instead, he'd taken him out onto Orchard Rest's porch and walked back and forth till he quieted. Sylvie had even cried when they'd embraced a final time for who knew what a voyage would bring. Or was she remembering her own removal from her homeland when she'd been forced onto a ship, never to return?

"Promise me you'll write as soon as you arrive and tell us how you're faring," Sylvie said, drying her eyes and taking the baby back.

"In the meantime, I'll finish what remains doing on your house," Will told Bleu. "My boys can till the garden behind it come spring, the girls can sow seed, and then wall it in with brick."

Titus squared his shoulders and tried to smile. "I don't want to go with you but I'll miss you—both of you."

Brielle kissed his cheek and Bleu embraced him next. "Look after Pearl and Windigo and I'll reward you well when I return."

Now, far beyond the Rivanna River, Brielle stood on deck, trying to get her bearings, Nadine beside her in a cardinal-red shawl. York Town was a thriving place, overflowing with taverns and warehouses yet surprising her with a few fine shops. At the last they'd visited the chocolatier on Water Street, buying a brick of *Shaw's* cocoa before their departure.

"I never thought to board a ship again nor wanted to." Squinting in the sun's glare off the water, Nadine pulled the brim of her straw hat lower. "This will be a far pleasanter journey. At least I'm sure of our destination."

"I pray for calm seas." Brielle looked to York Town and wondered if she'd ever see it again. "To think you'll soon be reunited with your loved ones after so long."

"Only seeing beloved family again could convince me," Nadine replied. "And to think you are on your way to meet your French relations for the first time. Bravo, *cher ami.*"

Such a strange nautical world they'd entered. Barefooted sailors moved around them in all directions, performing tasks and talking or shouting in abrupt, abbreviated tones, occasionally giving them a glance. Were they the only women passengers? She'd heard some of the most superstitious mariners thought women aboard a bad omen, yet the ship's mermaid figurehead seemed to make a mockery of that.

Bleu spoke with the captain near the wheel. Broad of shoulder and tall, he stood in stark contrast to the squat, balding ship's master. Their cargo was indigo, grain, and lumber. Brielle could smell the fresh wood in the hold. With gulls careening and crying overhead, they soon weighed anchor, a cabin boy showing them their cramped quarters. Bunks were built into the wall where they placed their bedrolls, pillows, and blankets. She'd grown so used to the spaciousness of the cottage she'd nearly forgotten the *Rose and Crown's* attic. This was even smaller.

Brielle felt a momentary panic at being shut in with nary a window. "Perhaps we can spend as much time on deck as down here."

"If all is calm, *oui.*" Nadine untied her chin ribbons and set her hat aside. "Have you never sailed?"

"Never, though my parents spoke of their coming to America from England long ago. I remember my mother saying she was seasick."

Nadine's features softened in sympathy. "*La mal de mer* is truly miserable."

"You may feel a bit unsteady at first." Bleu stood in the doorway surveying their quarters in one appraising glance. "I'm across the passageway should you need me."

Brielle smiled her thanks as she listened to the groan of the ship's timbers under sail and the thump of sailors' feet on the quarterdeck above. Her own footing was shaky as the floor tilted slightly. Even Bleu leaned into the doorframe.

"We'll meet for supper in the captain's great cabin," he said, consulting the pocket watch Will had given him upon leaving. "I'll escort you there if you're hungry."

Supper seemed another challenge given she'd already lost her appetite. Was it possible to be queasy so soon?

Nadine began arranging her bedding in a bid to lie down and Brielle did the same, setting the Bible Sylvie had given her on a table near the bunk. She opened it to another Psalm that seemed fitting for their watery endeavor.

If I take the wings of the morning, and dwell in the uttermost parts of the sea; Even there shall thy hand lead me, and thy right hand shall hold me.

24

$\mathcal{J}$ust when Brielle found her footing, a gale stole her hopes for the voyage and left her too sick to be terrified, violently ill to the point she thought she might die. Nadine and Bleu tended her when they weren't off their feet themselves. Bleu recovered first, able to enjoy being on deck in fair weather when he wasn't watching over her, his concern as touching as it was unnecessary.

The *Courageux* finally swept into French waters after five chancy weeks. On a blustery September day, beneath sapphire skies, they saw land as the sun shone down on a coastline considerably cooler than Virginia's. At last, Bleu led them off the ship and into Nantes, a sprawling, chaotic city made more confusing by the different languages sounding all around them. A veritable Tower of Babel.

Not far from the docks was the River Loire and the *auberge* where they'd stay till they made their next plans. *The White Cross* looked medieval but proved a refuge with clean, commodious rooms. Despite his Acadian patois, Bleu soon had them comfortably lodged, but only after an hour of waiting for their *letter de passe* from French authorities enabling them to travel.

The inn sat in the shadow of the *Château des Ducs de Bretagne*—the castle of the Dukes of Brittany—a massive granite hulk boasting towers, moat, and drawbridge. Cast back to the fairytales of her youth, Brielle half expected to see a damsel, knight, and dragon amid all that grey stone.

Though unutterably grateful to be on land, she was seized with a sudden homesickness for the familiar sights and sounds along the Rivanna, particularly the peace she'd found in the riverside chapel. There were churches here, too, small and large, just vastly different than America's. Nantes was layered and dense and centuries old whereas the colonies were young and raw and expansive.

Once they'd changed, they met for supper in the lively common room. Brielle couldn't complain about the fare or the small miracle that her appetite was returning. Hefty servings of roast mutton seasoned with fragrant herbs, boiled vegetables, and crusty *boule* served with butter and cheese made them forget the ship's stale biscuits and salted cod. She ate carefully, savoring every bite, careful not to overtax her still sore stomach. All of them were a tad thinner than when they'd left Virginia, and a ravenous Bleu seemed determined to reverse that.

"Have some *tarte aux pommes* with *crème*," Bleu encouraged, passing dessert.

Brielle eyed such richness warily along with the coffee he drank, a thick, black brew that smelled like burnt wood. She wanted nothing more than a cup of tea, the latter which he managed adroitly without her even asking.

She gazed at the stoneware cup and breathed in the scent of oolong. The attentive tavern maid even brought sugar. Brielle smiled her thanks, contentment stealing through her, as she met Bleu's eyes across the table and found them shining with relief.

Every protective instinct Bleu had reared up and left him determined to regain all that Brielle had lost on the rough journey.

If it had been any longer he wasn't sure she'd have made it. Another reason for her to remain in France. A return voyage might finish her.

Though he'd regained his feet fairly soon at sea, his own passage was so fraught with regret and apprehension that it marred his own enjoyment of the maritime world he found fascinating. He'd not been much beyond *Baie Francaise* in Acadie though he'd portaged and plied many inland waters. Much of Canada's wilderness was known to him but the Atlantic was a world apart.

"You shall turn me plump as a partridge," Brielle teased as if to alleviate his obvious concern.

"We will stay right here till you regain your strength." Looking at Nadine, he added, "After supper I'll make inquiries about your family."

Nadine pushed away her empty plate with a satisfied sigh, as spirited as Brielle was spent. "I shan't rest till you do."

He pondered their next move as Brielle sipped her tea to the music of a fiddle and flute in a far corner while patrons ate and smoked and conversed.

She seemed a bit lost as she gazed out a large bank of windows, the Nantes sun sinking to the west. "I didn't expect this city to be so grand."

"Twice the size of Philadelphia," he told her. "Good reason for you to stay close to me. I have signed you in as Madame Galant, besides."

Her smile, so seldom seen of late, turned his heart over. Though she didn't say another word he read much in her eyes. Could she read much in his? They held hers a fraction too long for propriety's sake though he, *un sauvage canadien*, hardly bent to civility.

"I suppose I shall pretend to be Madame Galant's lady's maid," Nadine jested.

He winked. "At least till you're reunited with your family."

The next day Nadine found her family on the outskirts of Nantes and, once they'd seen her safely settled, Brielle walked about the city with Bleu. When they happened upon a mantua maker's shop as well as a tailor's, one of dozens in the city, they tarried. Being a mecca for imported Indian chintzes and painted Chinese silks, warehouses were available to purchase ready-made garments. Surrounded by so many sumptuous choices, Brielle felt she'd stepped into a fairytale. They emerged hours later with parcels in arms and more to follow, hiring sedan chairs to navigate the narrow, crowded, and often filthy streets.

"And I thought my Lyonnaise silk would be enough," Brielle told him as they reached their lodging and climbed the stairs to their rooms. "How is it possible for you to finance my entire wardrobe—and yours besides?"

"Possible?" Bleu chuckled. "For most of my life I have wandered the North American wilderness. Eating in the wilds and sleeping in the open requires very little coin."

"And now you'll exchange your rustic garb for tailored garments." A far cry from the frontiersman he'd been when they'd first met.

He balanced their parcels and opened her door besides. "Next week should find us ready."

"Ready to go upriver and meet the *comte*?" Her eyes widened. Next week seemed too soon. "Shall we send word ahead of our coming?"

He hesitated. "The element of surprise might be best."

She wondered. Perhaps being warned of their coming increased their chances of being turned away. "Will we go by carriage?"

"*Non,* by barge or pinnace."

She sighed in dismay. "Another boat?"

"On a placid river." His eyes held hers in what seemed a promise. "No *mal de mer.*"

No more seasickness. And a few more blessed days, just the two of them. "What shall we do till then?"

"Visit the *Jardin des Plantes*?" He deposited their purchases on the table in her room. "Promenade along the River Loire or cross to the island of *Feydeau* and see the splendors along the *Rue Kervégan*? Anywhere or anything you fancy."

"You speak as if you've been here before."

His sturdy shoulders lifted in a shrug. "I ask questions of the residents because I'm intent on squiring you about."

"So I shall be Madame Galant awhile longer." She couldn't keep the teasing nor the wistfulness from her tone.

"I think you rather enjoy the role." His eyes lit in that way they did for no one else.

She had that, at least. His devotion. An undeniably fierce devotion. As for herself, she felt like she was merely playing dress-up when what she most wanted was to be his in more than name.

"Gabrielle Farrow Galant for the time being, *oui.*" His gaze swiveled to the hallway as footsteps signaled another lodger. "You are meant for more, *ma chérie.*"

"Let me be the judge of that," she replied softly before shutting her door.

25

A week—*une semaine*—passed far too quickly and they left Nantes, if only for a few hours. As they boarded a barge on the River Loire, Brielle held tight to her mother's jewelry box, her damp palms beneath her buttoned taffeta gloves the only indication of her skittishness. She looked to her flesh-and-blood anchor in his finely tailored buff and black garments, his hair carefully coiffed back with black silk ribbon, a new tricorn hat decorated with blue braid pulled low across his brow.

Appearances were everything, or so their attire seemed to say.

Bleu regarded her with concern and undisguised admiration. Elegantly clad from tip to toe in a new Indian chintz frock and matching hat, she felt far removed from the colonial she'd been. When he sat down beneath the fringed canopy beside her their cologne collided in a fragrant rush, his faint masculine *Eau de la Reine d'Hongrie* and her effusive feminine *Eau de Millefleurs*.

"*Château de Villandry* isn't far being on the lower Loire." Bleu spoke quietly, both of them facing forward, the oarsmen expertly steering the long vessel. "I have made discreet inquiries ... prepare to be *enchanté*."

"'Tis *bon*, then."

"Royal. The gardens are renowned."

"To think my mother fled this." Already she was awed by the landscape unfolding on both sides of them as the serpentine river swept them forward. Extensive vineyards covered rolling hillsides, the laborers tending them thick as bees.

"October is the harvest," he told her. "The region's wine is shipped to the colonies and beyond. Muscadet, especially."

Quaint villages sprouted like mushrooms, each centered around a tall-spired church while orchards and gardens boasted the last of the season's blooming. What must they be like in the lushness of spring or midsummer? On top of rises and along the very riverbanks sat *châteaux*, fairytale castles like those she'd only seen in paintings or read about in books. She was unprepared for all the beauty and grandeur—and her own bittersweet reaction to the sights and smells and sounds of her mother's former life.

"All this makes me forget what I want to say once I meet the *comte*," she said a bit breathlessly before abandoning English. "*Monsieur, je suis l'enfant unique de Josseline Vérany, votre fille. Je suis venu d'Amerique pour vous rencontrer si vous me permettez l'honneur.*"

Spoken in her most flawless if halting *français*, practiced so many times she could nearly say it in her sleep, and Bleu had not helped her. The words had come from her heart, crafted by her newfound wish to have a family, to know where she came from if only in part.

Overcome, she reached out and took his large hand in hers, a clasp of friendship in that moment. He squeezed her gloved fingers, his profile stoic though she sensed the tumult of his own thoughts and emotions beneath.

Within half an hour they swept round another watery bend to a poplar-lined bank, a warm wind stirring the tall trees and her hat ribbons. The barge slowed, the oarsmen poling toward a stone dock. An ornate iron fence was in back of it, immense ornamental gardens and pebbled walkways visible through its scrolled design.

Bleu handed her onto solid ground and Brielle stood trans-fixed, her gaze rising to a *château* of white stonework, glittering windows, and a steep slate roof. Ornamental vines softened the stony exterior with turrets she quickly numbered eight. A liveried porter stood by the fence and Bleu approached him, speaking in low tones while she waited.

"*Entrez*," the man told them, opening the gate.

Once admitted, she and Bleu began a slow walk along an avenue of manicured lime trees and box hedges, past a splash-ing fountain, occasionally pausing to admire flowers laid out in geometrical, color-coordinated squares. Hectares and hectares of gardens, each seeming to have a theme, pebbled walkways con-necting them.

Bleu plucked a creamy cabbage rose from a flowering bush and presented it to her like a seasoned courtier.

"You are bold, *monsieur*." She breathed in the exquisite blos-som's fragrance. "I have a feeling we're being watched from a hun-dred windows."

"By an army of servants, *oui*."

"To think my mother once walked these grounds ..."

A footman stood by a *château* door, clad like the porter by the river gate. Bleu walked ahead of her to speak to him in low tones. What he said to gain entry was a mystery but the door opened and they found themselves in a marble corridor, cool, shadowed, and still. A tall, bewigged man came toward them, his step brisk, his expression unreadable. He stopped to confer with the footman before showing them into a chamber as sumptuous as the gardens.

"*Le comte de Sancerre* is currently out riding," he said, introduc-ing himself as the estate's steward. "While you wait, I will arrange for refreshments to be brought."

"*Merci.*" Together they thanked him and stood in silence as the door shut behind him.

So, Grandfather still lived. She turned toward Bleu who was already looking at her as if weighing her reaction. She reached into her pocket for a hand fan. Though the room wasn't hot her skittishness was making her so.

Refreshments were brought on a silver tray and set down near a tall vase of damask roses. The presentation was so perfect she hated to disturb it. Orgeat to drink, fresh-picked fruit, madeleines, nutmeats, bread and *chèvre*. Neither of them seemed inclined to eat, but out of an unspoken respect for their host Bleu sampled everything while Brielle managed a few sips.

"I'm glad he's out riding. It gives me more time to collect myself." She took another drink of the oversweet orgeat. "Did you tell the servants who I am?"

"I merely said you are a relation."

"Now that we're here, I'm remembering bits and pieces of what my mother told me, namely that her father was formidable and may have viewed her departure as a betrayal." She looked toward a closed window, craving fresh air. "Growing older may have sharpened his temper."

"We're about to find out," he murmured, looking up at the ornate ceiling. "And I have no doubt you'll handle it with your usual grace."

"I don't want to disappoint you ... or myself." As it was, she wanted to fall headlong into his arms, run back to the barge, and return downriver to Nantes. "I have little else but your prayers and presence to steady me."

"You'll face him alone, understand." He held her gaze, compassion in his eyes. "Such a private moment should be between the two of you and no one else."

She nodded, hearing footsteps in the hall. "You'll be right here, waiting, no matter what."

It wasn't a question but he answered it anyway. "I'll be waiting, *oui*. For however long it takes."

"*Mademoiselle* ..." The unsmiling steward reappeared, gesturing for her to follow. "*Le Comte de Sancerre* has returned and awaits you in the Grand Salon."

As Brielle's footsteps faded, Bleu sensed she was beginning to move far beyond his reach. The realization tugged at him so hard he found it hard to breathe. Atop the mantel the gilt clock's hands seemed to freeze. His gaze roamed the vermillion damask walls where everything appeared to be in a state of splendid perfection devoid of even a speck of dust.

The vaulted ceiling was a masterpiece of stucco, an expansive fresco of the heavens complete with angelic beings in gold leaf. A crystal chandelier hung at the room's center, its crystals scattering light from a wall of windows.

His own humble house along the Rivanna seemed a hovel. Once a source of pride and satisfaction, it now filled him with a dismay bordering on disgust. How had he ever thought it would be good enough for a bride—Brielle? Now, having set foot in *Château de Villandry*, he would carry the comparison to his grave.

With a start he realized she'd forgotten her jewelry box. She'd set it down to take the glass of orgeat and forgotten it. Perhaps it wasn't needed. The portrait on its lid proved her to be her mother's daughter beyond all doubt.

Restless, he moved to a window triple his height, autumn sunlight streaming through spotless mullioned panes. A chair rested by the ledge. He dare not sit down. He was not a small man, and the gilded seat looked to have been built for a nymph or ethereal fairy.

Everything here seemed dreamlike, so far removed from the world he knew it made him strangely weary. Even genteel Virginia seemed a scattering of dust, Canada raw, endless wilderness. He didn't belong here. His immaculate, tailored clothing—the powdered wig he refused to wear—the garish buckled shoes on his feet all seemed laughable.

If he'd been cast in a farce he couldn't feel more ridiculous. He was playacting on behalf of Brielle To reunite her with her family. To ensure her rightful place. His qualms about her grandfather's reception were small. One look at her and he would capitulate in a breath. It had happened to him the first time he'd met her.

Enchanteresse.

26

$\mathscr{B}$ rielle walked into a salon adorned in every hue of blue, so captivated she nearly missed the man waiting by a marble hearth at one end. Still in his riding garb, his graying head came no higher than the mantel. When the steward exited and closed the door, she approached the *comte* though it took a great many steps on unsteady legs to cross the large, carpeted room.

She felt a flicker of panic, remembering her jewelry box. Too late. When she paused at a respectful distance, she curtsied. She'd practiced that, too, in the privacy of her Nantes room till her movements were seamless and elegant, or so she hoped.

Smile, bend the knee, slide one foot and cross the ankles, lower and lift her skirts.

When she straightened the sun seemed to shift, catching the *comte* in a shaft of light through a near window, illuminating the sudden confusion and then the stunned clarity on his lined face.

"*Sacrebleu …*" he murmured.

He regarded her a moment longer before he turned and went through a door disguised in a paneled wall she hadn't even realized was there. It shut behind him and she heard him weeping.

Weeping.

What had she done?

The tender moment bespoke regret, a lifetime of missing another, years spent wondering. Fumbling for her handkerchief, she dried her own eyes, unsure what to do next, when the door reopened and he reappeared.

The lines on the *comte's* angular face were carved deep, his eyes the hue of her own, his features echoing her mother's. In the utterly awkward moment, she nearly forgot what she'd meant to say and the words came out in a staccato rush—

"Sir, I am the only child of Josseline Vérany, your daughter. She no longer lives but I have come from America to meet you if you will allow me the honor."

The clumsy statement brought the room to a standstill all over again. Never had a moment been so painfully poignant. Slowly, he moved toward her as if she was ethereal as a phantom and might vanish. Touching her arm gently, he turned her around. At the end of the room on the far wall was a painting of a young woman they had both loved and lost. Before Brielle could study the canvas with any appreciation, his hand fell away and he left the room again without a word.

The steward appeared instead, ushering her back to Bleu with a formal unapologetic excuse. "*Mademoiselle*, the *comte* is overcome and cannot meet with you further."

Numb, she let Bleu take charge. He thanked the steward and they retraced their steps, walking wordlessly and woodenly through the gardens toward the gate and waiting barge. All the while Brielle replayed the brief moments alone with the *comte* in tortuous detail, wishing she had done things differently, perhaps given him some sort of warning before her appearing.

Riven with regret, she took a last look at the *château's* façade as the river swept them out of sight toward Nantes.

They dined at *Le Grand Monarque* on *Rue du Marchix* in Nantes. One of the most celebrated establishments in the city, it was not far from the inn where they were staying. Sunset gilded the city's spires and rooftops and balconettes as it faded to the west. The dying day would soon be over, its humbling memories with it, or so Bleu hoped.

He ordered for them at a corner table to one side of a cavernous, flickering hearth. Though the autumn days were warm, the nights were cool. He doubted Brielle would eat, her appetite likely stolen by what had happened. Clutching her jewelry box, she'd hardly said a word on the way downriver. Now, as they waited for their meal, she sipped a cup of Marseilles tea and began to talk.

"I hardly know where to begin ..." She stirred more sugar into her cup absently. "The *comte* was clearly overcome. He pointed to my mother's portrait on the salon wall then left the room again. After that, the steward came to tell me he could not see me any longer and ended the matter."

Bleu studied her, feeling she'd stepped toward him again instead of away from him.

"I was so emotional in that moment that our meeting is a blur." Her gaze stayed troubled. "I'm sorry I caused him more pain. I don't think I reckoned with the toll of telling him who I was and *Maman's* death all at once."

True, the old man might have cherished the hope of reuniting with his daughter one day. "Perhaps I erred and should have sent word upriver first."

"It may not have helped." Her eyes glistened again. "Any meeting under the circumstances is fraught."

"Are you sorry we came?" He nearly held his breath waiting for her answer.

"*Non*," she said firmly. "I have experienced a treasured part of my mother's past. Perhaps that is enough."

Enough? He'd hoped there'd be instant acceptance, an invitation, but all had been a gamble and now nothing had been gained but their short-lived reunion. Perhaps too much time had passed. Clearly the *comte* had lived a life without his daughter and entirely without his granddaughter. He might not want to change that, harsh as it was.

Supper was served—beef ragout and a cheese souffle, salat, bread, and fruit. To his surprise Brielle ate everything as if she'd already put the episode behind her while he hadn't much appetite. As for himself, seeing her in her lovely gown and hat, their idyllic ride beneath the canopy on the barge, and this satisfying meal was something he'd remember for the rest of his life.

She smiled and poured herself another cup of tea as if she'd dealt with the day and dismissed it. Or was she simply trying to put on a brave front and bolster him? "I am ready to return to the Rivanna."

"*Sacré Dieu.*" He set down his knife and fork, trying to keep his surprise and pleasure in check. "Already?"

"*Oui.* Tomorrow, if you can arrange it."

Her haste was amusing. He almost laughed. "It might take a few days more."

"Then we'll continue to enjoy the sights of Nantes till then." She all but winked at him. "And keep pretending to be Monsieur and Madame Galant."

"You're taking this well, *mon bonheur.*"

"Don't you miss it? Virginia, I mean."

Did he? He'd seldom formed such attachments since Acadie. He let that digest along with his meal as he finished what was on his plate and she drained the teapot. Occasionally she stole a shy, almost coquettish look at him.

Suddenly he felt *he* was being courted. The possibility caught him off guard. Her ongoing regard of him as her hero was something he'd thought would pass. But a rough ocean voyage and today's events seemed only to have fueled her devotion. And the warmth building inside him was something he could no longer ignore.

"As for Virginia …" He finished his wine. "We need to see if Nadine is ready to leave for the colonies or stay on."

But Nadine was the furthest thing from his mind. His main concern was Brielle. He didn't want to subject her to another rough crossing so soon. Perhaps the better plan was to confess how he felt about her, propose marriage right here and if she would have him honeymoon on the idyllic isle of *Feydeau*. If they tired of that, which he doubted, they could go to Paris and spend the remainder of his monies, saving just enough for their return passage to Virginia.

Perhaps he needed France as much as she did, if only to clear his head and help him gain a different perspective after nearly a decade of war and upheaval. Once he returned to America, what then? He must decide whether to resume his work for the colonial government or commit to the Rivanna settlement and stay on in his nearly finished house.

But that hinged almost entirely on Brielle and what happened here.

They spent the next morning at the city's market, strolling among the colorful stalls and carts, Brielle with a basket on one arm like so many Nantes *mesdames*. Given the fact he hadn't proposed their staying on in France, their thoughts turned toward Virginia as they selected cheese from Normandy, olives from Provence, and Bordeaux wine as gifts for Sylvie and Will. Dolls and miniature furniture sufficed for the girls and puzzles and the game *jeu de l'oie*

for the boys, even an amber teething rattle for the *enfant*. Another trunk was needed to carry Chantilly lace, silk, and woolen camlet and serge, as well as a variety of embroidery threads and ribbons.

"My sister will no doubt welcome us home," he jested as his wallet emptied.

Brielle looked a bit wistful admiring a shop window. Baubles and trinkets of all kinds winked back at them from one of the foremost Nantes jewelers. Was she thinking of her jewelry box and the necklace and ring she'd not been able to show her grandfather?

Arm in arm, they wound their way back to *The White Cross,* their purchases to be delivered on the morrow, yesterday's disappointment receding. Brielle yawned behind a gloved hand, saying she needed a nap while he wanted nothing more than a quiet corner and a newspaper or broadside with some word about the distant colonies.

Entering the inn's shadowed interior, they found it oddly empty save a liveried footman near the stairs. Bleu felt a tick of concern. The same footman they'd seen at the *château* yesterday? With a terse greeting, he presented Brielle with a letter. Thanking him, she broke the seal and read it silently before turning to Bleu in astonishment.

"What are we to do?" she asked.

He took it from her as the footman looked on, awaiting their decision. They'd been invited to the *château* as guests where the *comte* could get to know his granddaughter better. His personal barge awaited to return them and their belongings upriver.

Bleu folded the letter and handed it back to her. "A very gracious invitation."

Her perplexity deepened. "Shall we accept?"

We. The word heartened him. But now this extraordinary turn ...

He held her gaze and read a hesitant hope there as Virginia receded like the tide. "*Bien sûr.*"

Of course.

With a deferential nod, the footman followed them upstairs to retrieve their baggage. After an explanation to the innkeeper about their unplanned departure and the goods they'd purchased that would be delivered on the morrow, they left. The journey upriver seemed far swifter than yesterday, the *comte's* barge more elegantly appointed.

Whatever awaited, Bleu hoped it would keep them together rather than drive them apart.

27

*B*rielle stepped into the lavender suite she'd been given on the *château's* second floor as footmen brought up her embarrassingly beleaguered baggage. Her slippers sank into the floral carpet as she took in the rooms—bedchamber, *boudoir, garde-robe*, and salon—that seemed more indoor garden, fresh bouquets of flowers at every turn.

"Here you shall receive your visitors as French gentlewomen do," the maid, Cosette, told her, as she put away Brielle's belongings in an armoire the size of her room at the inn.

With a word that she'd return to help her dress for supper, Cosette disappeared, and Brielle stood in the sumptuous silence in disbelief. She wondered the *comte's* change of mind—and heart. She'd thought all was lost, their horrendous ocean voyage for naught, but the palatial windows facing the River Loire and gardens told her otherwise.

Purples of every hue adorned the chamber from the silk wall-coverings to the lofty bed with its exquisitely carved floral motif. The domed canopy—a crown of faux flowers—was suspended from the ceiling rather than supported on posts, its woven tapestried hangings the shade of lilacs. A high bed required bedsteps and boasted not one mattress but three, filled with feathers, and half a dozen pillows in embroidered slips.

A dressing table, twin to the carved bed, was arrayed with brushes, combs, powders, perfumes, and pomatum, even silk puffs. A selection of hand fans in decorative cases had the feel of the past. On one end of the dressing table rested the jewelry box she'd brought upriver. Beside it sat another larger case that took pride of place. Brielle opened it, astonished to find the velvet-lined space as full as hers was empty. A pearl necklace, jeweled hairpins, a diamond pendant, even a *lavalier* made of a gold chain and assorted gems were among them.

A writing desk sat beneath one window furnished with quills, ink, fine paper, and wax.

Had this been her mother's room?

Was Bleu's room as palatial?

She'd know at supper, she supposed, for that was when the *comte* had requested they join him. For now, exhilarated if exhausted, she lay down atop the bed and slept till Cosette returned to wake her and begin what would become a rather tiring toilette. For a colonial woman used to donning the simplest garments by herself and either braiding or thrusting a few pins into her hair to keep it subdued beneath a plain linen cap, she marveled.

Finally bathed, powdered, bewigged, and wearing the Lyonnaise silk dress Sylvie had remade for her, she met Bleu at the door of the dining room. His admiring gaze told her she was not as ill-clad as she feared, his eyes lingering on her coiffure bemusedly, a confection of curls and pale pink powder.

"Cosette's doing," she whispered, putting a hand to her wig. The maid had it so tightly pinned her scalp ached. Bleu's own hair was unpowdered, but his dark blue Nantes suit was exceedingly fine.

"I nearly got lost …" He smiled and offered her his arm as they went in to yet another glittering room. "And for a moment—when you came down the stairs—I doubted it was you."

"I shan't be wearing a wig again, no matter French custom." She looked around uncertainly. "Have you seen—" What should she call him? Not grandfather. Not yet. The *comte*, she guessed.

"Your *grand-père*? *Non*." Bleu turned back to her, looking as relaxed as he'd been along the Rivanna. "Perhaps it is French custom for the host to arrive last."

Brielle prepared herself for his return as well as what she guessed would be a bewildering number of French dishes. Another five minutes passed and the *comte* entered the room through a side door, far more composed than he'd been when they'd first met. Bleu bowed and Brielle curtsied as he came forward and kissed her on both cheeks.

"I am glad you have returned, the both of you," he said when they sat down at one end of a long, candlelit table. "Forgive me for not asking you to be my guests sooner. I was quite undone."

Brielle understood. She still felt undone. Undone by the grandeur, his sudden reversal, and even Bleu's presence as he sat across from her, Grandfather at the head of the table. She studied him in small snatches, noting all the little things that reminded her of her mother. His close-set eyes, the slant of his nose, even the timbre of his voice and its inflections. Small yet commanding, he was gracious. Observant. Astute.

She tamped down a thousand questions as supper was served. Bleu seemed more amused than bewildered at all the cutlery. Somehow, they avoided a *faux pas* and followed Grandfather's lead on which utensil to use, starting from the outside and moving inward toward the porcelain plate. Brielle lost count of the courses that finally ended with an airy meringue atop vanilla custard accompanied by coffee in delicate cups and followed by glasses of Armagnac.

The noisy, happy chatter of Sylvie and her family around Orchard Rest's table seemed hazy, the distant details nearly forgotten. Were all meals here so silent? Or perhaps the better question—

Was Grandfather accustomed to dining alone? Rather, was he lonely?

"Shall we stroll through the gardens and settle our supper?" he asked with a smile, rising from his chair once they'd finished. "They're well illuminated for walking."

They passed outside through French doors and down steps leading to graveled paths. Lanthorns hung from posts lighting their way. They walked slowly, listening as he spoke of the *château's* history and their family. Generations of names she'd never heard and couldn't possibly remember passed through her head even as her rich lineage left her somewhat awestruck.

She finally worked up the courage to say, "Tell me about my mother, *monsieur.*"

"Please call me *grand-père,*" he chided gently, pausing beside the largest fountain. "You've been given her bedchamber, *petite-fille.*"

"I thought so."

"Your mother was my life. Your *grand-mère's* life. We had a son and heir born two years after her birth. We had not thought to have any children after being married many years and so both of them were something of a miracle. Josseline grew up here on the River Loire and the gardens were her particular delight. When she left us at the age of twenty we felt it like a death."

"And Andre?" Her mother had only spoken of her brother once that Brielle could remember. The son and heir.

"Andre died five years after your mother left France. A riding accident."

The sorrow in his voice made her want to return to him all the years had taken. But how? Expressing her sympathy seemed a very small condolence no matter how heartfelt.

"*Maman* spoke of you often at our home in Philadelphia. She missed you and her life here even after she'd made her choice to be with my father."

"And now they are both gone, along with your beloved *grand-mère*." His eyes were damp but he didn't reach for a handkerchief. "When I saw you, you needn't have said a word. You are the living image of Josseline, so like the salon's painting."

"I would like to show *Monsieur* Galant," she said with sudden formality. In this grand house where she was still unsure of herself, she sensed etiquette must be observed. "I am so pleased you find me like her."

Grandfather nodded at Bleu. "Tell me, *monsieur*, about yourself. You are from a distant shore, perhaps a French-Canadian, a Métis. Your French dialect is different than ours on this side of the Atlantic."

"I am, at heart, a *coureur des bois*, a woods-runner."

"A remarkably well spoken one." Grandfather's surprise was evident. "And literate, it seems."

"Early on I was schooled by French priests in Acadie. After that, books have been my teachers," Bleu explained. "An interpreter and liaison must have a mastery of words, at least spoken. Spending time with countless military officers and officials also leaves a mark."

He told of his background, his years as a Hudson's Bay Trader and Resistance fighter before the British expulsion and the eight years following when he'd worked with various tribes and the British and French from Canada to colonial America. Never long-winded, he kept them rapt and added fresh details new to Brielle.

"You have endured much, *monsieur*. I see your scar. We have heard about the terrible atrocities inflicted by our enemy, England. Many lives lost on all sides." Grandfather looked as grieved as

Brielle felt. "You are as much in need of a respite as Gabrielle, no doubt."

"I agree," she said, telling their story and missing Titus afresh as they did so. "Even with all his losses this woods-runner took time to redeem two indentures or we'd still be indebted to an unscrupulous bondsman for years."

"I owe you as well as Gabrielle." Grandfather regarded Bleu with respect and gratitude. "If not for your selfless actions, even meeting my granddaughter would have been an impossibility. I want to recompense you fully." He looked at Brielle, his face alight with a joy that a reunion brings. "And now that you are here, shall we have a *fête*? You have a great many relatives—uncles, aunts, and cousins—who will be wanting to meet you."

"I've always wondered about family here," she told him. "My first French *fête*. A sweet prospect, thank you."

The next afternoon, Bleu rode out with the *comte* on a stallion that, fine as it was, made him wonder how Windigo was faring. Vaillant had been sired at the royal stables, *Les Haras Royaux*. Brielle was given her own mount—an elegant Andalusian from Spain—but today her time was better spent preparing for the *couturières*, that army of dressmakers who'd soon descend on the *château*, ready to dizzy Brielle with the newest fabrics and furbelows.

"I am in need of fresh air," the *comte* jested atop his own mount. "I have lived too long a widower and have quite forgotten the fuss and expense of the feminine sort."

They rode along the River Loire's heights where limestone bluffs offered dramatic views of the valley and beyond it. After so much time aboard ship and walking about the city, Bleu regained a freedom he'd lost.

"You are an expert horsemen, *monsieur*. Something tells me you could ride to Paris and back without breaking your stride."

Bleu ran a gloved hand along the stallion's mane. "My Acadian father—Gabriel Galant—had as many horses as cattle. I've spent much of my life astride though I've never ridden as fine a mount as Vaillant."

"Few can manage Vaillant, a testament to your skill." His knowing smile revealed he was thinking of something else entirely. "You also excel as an escort to my granddaughter though I do sense something more at play."

"On my part if not hers, *Monsieur le Comte*." Bleu slowed his horse to a walk, eyes on a distant church spire amid hectares of vineyards. "I assure you my intentions are undeclared—and honorable."

"I do not doubt it. But surely there is more …"

For once, Bleu had no words. How could he explain without sounding grandiose his belief that he'd been charged with Brielle's keeping for a time? That in a small, almost holy way he was entrusted with something infinitely precious that even he did not understand?

"I've come to believe our meeting was no accident," he finally said. "That I am simply a means to an end for her, if only to reunite her with you."

"You, Galant, have a gallantry and generosity of spirit many lack. A singular purpose."

"I simply want what is best for her. She is alone in the colonies, without kin. She deserves a better life, a family. A secure future."

"And you cannot provide her with that?"

Bleu gestured to their surroundings with a gloved hand. "I have little to offer compared to this."

"Yet you have refused my offer of reimbursement. What *can* I do for you?"

"My concern is for Brielle, not myself." His hopes for her made him bold as did his standing—or the lack of it. France's protocols and proprieties had no hold on him. "Welcome her as your granddaughter. Never let her feel less than the noblewoman she is. Treat her as if nothing has divided you."

"And where does that leave you?"

"For now I am your grateful guest. I'll return to America in time."

The *comte* studied him gravely. "What or who do you have there?"

"My sister and her family. My fellow Acadians." Bleu looked west. "And if I ever return to Canada there are my mother's people, the Mi'kmaq."

"I do not think my granddaughter will take your leaving lightly."

"Some goodbyes are necessary, even inevitable, and I have had many." Bleu's easy reply belied what he was feeling. Saying *adieu* to Brielle would be the thorniest of all. "Life is a series of farewells and partings, some harder than others."

"Spoken like a French philosopher."

They rode on, the *comte* pointing out points of interest and telling the Loire's ancient, battle-scarred history. Returning to the *château* in the early afternoon, the *comte* had business to attend to and Bleu found himself in the library, wanting to fill his hours well when Brielle was occupied elsewhere. He happened upon a copy of *Robinson Crusoe* and *Gulliver's Travels*, two novels he'd enjoyed before but were worth a second reading.

He took a chair by a window, only to come to his feet again when Brielle entered, her face aglow. "There you are. The tailor will be here for you soon."

"*Tailleur?*"

"I'm not the only one who needs dressing, remember. Grandfather insists on a new wardrobe for us both at his expense—and no expense is to be spared. Not even our Nantes fashions will do."

"French fashion is a far cry from colonial America, *non?*" He set the books aside. "Rather like a crystal chandelier to a candle stub."

"Quite." She laughed. "Hours and hours with the *couturières* has finally made me feel more a peacock than a potato sack."

"You have never been guilty of the latter," he said with feeling. In fact, he preferred her in simple linen, not silk, though she wore both well.

She flushed. "But before the tailor, we must have *thé.*"

"And what is that?" he teased, knowing full well what awaited.

She took his arm as they left the library and descended wide stone steps into the parterre garden with its reflecting pools. Down an *allée* stood the orangerie she loved, a glass structure brimming with potted citrus trees and exotic plants. She pointed out a still-blooming oleander in one corner as a breeze pushed against them with a hint of cooler weather to come. Autumn had been unseasonably warm, coaxing the gardens into another blooming. At the heart of the glass structure a small table had been set with *sèvres* china, a footman standing by.

"Such extravagance." Bleu sat down in an upholstered chair, the orangeries' scent like perfume. "Do you mean to civilize me?"

"I hope not." She smiled back at him. "I prefer you just as you are."

"All this makes me wonder what my fellow woods-runners would think."

"You're not missing your former life, I hope."

He chuckled. "There is simply no time for that, *mon cher.*"

A footman served then bowed out when Brielle thanked him. Together they surveyed the pastries and confections crowding the silver tray between them. Her delight made him want to pretend to enjoy it too, but what he craved was a ripe Rivanna orchard apple.

"Shall we say grace?" She reached for his hand across the table. "Or as Sylvie says—*grâce au bon Dieu*."

He leaned in and took her extended fingers when what he wanted was to take her in his arms. She seemed to be changing moment by moment and bore no resemblance to the young woman he'd met months ago. In her painted silk, she didn't resemble a *comte's* granddaughter but a *princesse*. All she lacked was a tiara or a crown. And he had to grudgingly admit she looked as at home here as he felt at sea.

They bowed their heads, and he uttered a simple French prayer learned long ago from his adopted French-Acadian mother. "Bless us, Heavenly Father, and bless this food, those who prepared it, and provide bread to those who have none. Amen."

"Amen," she echoed, placing her serviette in her lap. "We must sit down and catch our breath from time to time and give thanks."

Her *we* was worrisome. As if they were more than a lady and her escort. As for catching her breath ... "Are you having any qualms?"

"About being here?" She smiled as if to reassure him. "How can one complain about so much bounty and beauty?"

He caught the slight hesitation in her voice. "But ..." He held her gaze.

"Sometimes I'm unsettled. A bit overawed."

"Natural, *non*?"

"Perhaps. But you don't appear to feel the same."

"I am used to being in shifting circumstances, always on the move, never knowing what will happen next. This is simply another one of them. I navigate it and go on."

"I miss the peace and simplicity of the Rivanna."

"Perhaps in hindsight it is unreasonably idyllic." Even as he said it he could think of few flaws. "You weren't there long enough to discover its faults."

"Name them."

"And shatter your illusions?" He chuckled and reached for a confection. "*Non.*"

She turned her attention to the sweets rather absently. "I miss the chapel and my little cottage … the sound of the settlement bell …. the river's rush and the view of the mountains from your porch—"

"Careful. You'll make me homesick."

"Is the Rivanna home to you, then?" Hope shone in her eyes. "More than Acadie, even?"

He looked at her but had no answer. Acadie's absence created a longing that defied words and hadn't abated. He wanted to feel the same way she did about the Rivanna—only without her, if he must return alone. There was no denying its peace and simplicity.

"I hear you're enjoying riding about the countryside." Pensive, she stirred cream and sugar into her tea. "My fear is that France will woo you away from me and I'll rarely see you except for meals."

"Three times a day is not enough?" he jested. "So you add *thé?*"

After much pondering, she selected a lemon tart. "I breakfast in my rooms, remember."

He usually breakfasted with the *comte,* rather formal affairs with a host of attentive servants doing everything but placing the serviettes in their laps. But her grandfather was good company, always asking about his exploits and easily entertained with tales of Canada's white spirit bears and all the ways the Resistance had thwarted the British.

He brushed a crumb off his riding coat. "How are you spend-ing your time?"

"Our rather quiet but full schedule is about to change, Grandfather tells me. After the *faire la fête* invitations will pour in."

He resisted a groan. "But for now?"

"For now, after breakfast, I dress and go to chapel for morning prayers. Reading and letters take up the forenoon—I'm writing to Sylvie now—and then we meet for *déjeuner* at midday, as you know. Afterwards I spend time with Grandfather in his study followed by embroidery or painting or learning the pianoforte. I often walk about the gardens or go to the stables for a ride accompanied by a groom and sometimes Grandfather. Then I dress for *dîner* ..."

"Don't forget dance lessons."

"Oh, yes. Sorely needed though I shall never master the minuet." She looked at him intently. "How are you spending your hours?"

"It is hard work being a gentleman." He expelled a breath, his tone faintly mocking. "Mornings are for reading the newspapers and drinking strong coffee. Then I visit the stables and ride until the midday meal which threatens to burst my buttons. Afterwards I take a boat upriver to watch the harvest at your grandfather's vineyards or walk in the woods. I've tried archery with some suc-cess and now have a fencing master."

"So I've heard. Grandfather is astonished at your skill."

"Swords and knives are known to me but not French formali-ties and their codes of honor."

"Perhaps I shall take up fencing myself as a female, in the style of *Julie d'Aubigny* or *Chevalier d'Eon*.

He chuckled, nearly spilling his tea. "You could be my spar-ring partner, then."

"Fencing aside, even the servants boast of your marksman-ship," she told him. "A footman said you hit a crown piece tossed into the air with the armory's best pistols."

"Did I?" He cupped the delicate porcelain with one sinewy hand. "And you are rapidly recovering your French."

"*Grand-père* refuses to speak English. He says it taxes his brain."

"I would agree. French is as natural to him as Mi'kmaq is to me."

She took another pastry. "I've never heard you speak it except for naming Windigo. Perhaps it's time to teach me a few words and phrases."

"Where to begin ..." Her earnestness made him continue. "*Ge'nnu'-gluli* means 'speak to me' in Mi'kmaq." She echoed him and he continued, "*E'e* would be your reply."

She stirred more cream into her cup. "How do you say thank you?"

"*Wela'lin.*"

"Goodbye?"

"*Nmultis.*"

She repeated each thoughtfully, sipping tea between questions. "And ... I love you?"

He held her gaze, his insides swirling despite his stoicism. "*Kesalul.*"

"*Kesa ... lul.*"

"*Kesalul,*" he repeated slowly as the feeling between them pulsed to new heights. If the table wasn't between them ...

"Your first language is like nothing I've ever heard," she said quietly. "Very unique and beautiful."

He was the first to look away, his tea forgotten. "Once we've finished here, why don't you show me the portrait of your mother."

"Very well." She gave him a smile, still looking wistful—and making him wonder what she felt soul deep.

28

hey finally stood before the portrait of Josseline Vérany. The salon was hushed, the emotion between them still high. Bleu was no longer studying the magnificent portrait but Brielle. Once again he fisted his hands behind his back to keep from reaching for her.

"Your mother was a beautiful woman ..." he said. "But you are even moreso."

Brielle seemed to hardly hear him, absorbed as she was in the painting. "Grandfather said this was commissioned on the eve of her first *fête*. Soon after that she met my father. *Maman* was happy here in France, but she was happiest with him."

"Theirs was a love match, then."

"Blessedly so." She turned back to him. "I wish you could have met them. They would have been very fond of you."

"For rescuing their daughter as you say."

"For being the selfless, noble soul that you are."

"I am far from perfect, *mon cher*."

She touched the canvas, running a finger along the yellow of her mother's gown that seemed more silk than oil paint. "Grandfather wants me to have my portrait painted so that it hangs opposite her."

Bleu looked over his shoulder to the far end of the room and saw a bare damask wall.

"He's already commissioned Maurice-Quentin de La Tour for the task."

"Task?" He fisted his hands harder. "More privilege."

She turned toward him, her hands clasped at her sashed waist. "Will you sit for a miniature, one I can keep in my bodice or pocket? To remember our time here?"

The request seemed bittersweet. "I'll have no trouble remembering our time here. But I do have trouble sitting still." His resistance died when she smiled at him again. "But for you …"

"*Merci.* Monsieur de La Tour will arrive after the *fête.*" She pulled a tiny, gold timepiece from her pocket, a gift from the *comte.*

Watching her, he thought of life before France. Of boundless, unfettered time. Freedom.

"The dancing master is coming soon." She looked at him again, expectant. "Will you be there?"

"Only if we avoid the minuet."

"We shall. I'm much more fond of the gavotte and allemande and cotillion."

"Don't forget the *bourré* we stepped along the Rivanna."

"I shan't." Her gaze grew almost starry again. "Everything about that night seems gilded to me."

"*This* is gilded." He looked about the salon and wondered about the ballroom he'd not seen yet. Wondered, too, if he'd have a chance to partner with her again. An onslaught of suitors were about to descend. He felt it to his marrow.

She touched his sleeve. "Promise me a dance like last time."

He focused on the portrait rather than her. "If one is open, *oui.*"

"It will be open, I promise."

He looked at her again. Her rose cologne encircled him, making him want to remove the pearl comb that had nearly slipped free of her coiffure and bury his face in her unbound hair, every mahogany-gold strand. A far cry from the braided maid he'd rescued. He was having trouble reconciling the woman she'd been to the one she was becoming. The Brielle of old felt within his reach, the other an impossibility. A dream.

He'd brought her here. Only now did he realize the plan had been more his than hers. He believed she belonged in France, the place of her heritage. Only his love for her hadn't ebbed, only surged. He not only loved her, he was willing to die for her. He'd never cared for anyone so much nor had he reckoned with the cost of releasing her.

Non, imbécile. Fight!

The urge came unbidden and soul deep. Fight for what might be lost, for what was fleeting. For a home across the sea and a loving woman who kept him there. For their future, their children, their legacy. A knifelike anguish twisted inside him. His heart beat so hard surely she heard it.

As if sensing his inner struggle, she reached up and touched his cheek. The scar that marred his brow to his jawline was no longer an angry crimson but faded by time. Years had passed since he'd fought and lost Acadie. In another decade would he recall this very moment with the same aching, irreversible wrench? If he didn't fight for her—for what they had—the scar to his heart would be far worse.

He took a deep breath and covered her fingers with his own. "Brielle ..."

A sudden voice sounded from the salon's open double doors and her feather-light fingers fell away. Their privacy fled.

"You look as though you're about to dance." The *comte's* smile softened his features. "I would join you if my rheumatic legs would allow it."

Brielle moved across the salon to kiss him on both cheeks. "We were admiring *Maman* and discussing the coming *fête* while awaiting the dance master."

"Ah, the masquerade ball that will last all night and introduce you to much of society except those unfortunates frolicking with the king and queen at Versailles."

"Is your ballroom big enough?" she asked as they moved toward Bleu.

"It can accommodate a few hundred," Grandfather replied. "Mercifully, there are many doors that open onto the terrace so guests can be outside in the fresh air should it become too crowded."

"Will you be my first dance, then, *grand-père*?" she asked, a smile in her voice. "My last is already taken."

The masked ball began beneath a full moon that turned the Loire into silver ribbon. The incessant sound of carriages on cobblestones reached Brielle in her suite. Stifling a yawn, she waited for the ordeal of dressing to be over as it seemed she'd been preparing since breakfast. Now evening and swathed in apricot silk and Chantilly lace, she turned before a looking glass to admire the garment that rivaled Parisian gowns, the seamstress said. Half a dozen maids encircled her, ready to adjust, snip, and pin every part of her ensemble. Brielle lost track of who said what with their effusive chatter.

"Is it true American ladies prefer coiffures like yours?"

"Others may be powdered and puffed but you make the artificial unnecessary."

"You belong at the court of Versailles, *Mademoiselle*."

Cosette brought her half-mask, its edges adorned with the same Chantilly lace as her gown and embellished with faux gemstones and feathers.

No one knew who she was … including she herself.

She left her boudoir, the odd thought circling round her head as she caught her reflection in a hall mirror by the light of a hundred candles. Such extravagance. Such a charade. She still felt she was playing dress up, pretending to be someone she was not.

Grand-père was waiting, escorting her down the *château's* staircase to the ballroom now teeming with guests, the hubbub already so great she could hardly hear his remarks. Four hundred guests?

Where was Bleu?

All was a fascinating if bewildering blur of costumes—Venus in a rose-wreathed frock, Cupid with powdered pink hair, monks and friars and knights, harlequins and sailors, sultans and shepherdesses, kings and queens and clowns.

Her own mask was itchy against her already heated skin, and she resisted the urge to tear it free. "I suppose I have the extra advantage of being unknown to all."

"All they know is that a surprise is in store," Grandfather said, seemingly amused at the ruse. "At midnight when all unmask I shall introduce you."

And once her mask came off, the imposter she was—the orphaned, indentured tavern maid with callused hands—would be revealed. Or so she felt. These guests had nothing to hide, all aristocrats to the core.

Musicians tuned their instruments as the ballroom filled. Brielle stood by open double doors as the opening minuet ensued and then, despite the challenge of new shoes and being half-masked, partnered with Grandfather for a gavotte. A performance—for that is what it was—every eye on them, especially her, the mysterious stranger. The crowd's swelling merriment gladdened and drained her all at once, but the press of guests seemed incomplete as she searched and discarded the costumed men in the immense room.

None compared to Bleu.

Frustration sparked. Had he decided not to attend? Was he unwell? Or was it simply the fact he was disguised and somehow she overlooked him?

The air grew sullied by spirits and sweat, the laughter almost maniacal in places, the stares of so many unsettling. She drank a cup of punch, joined three other couples for a cotillion, her fully masked partner dressed as a Venetian, or so he told her. More dancing ensued, other partners trying to guess her identity and provoke her into removing her mask too soon.

In time they adjourned to the buffet—no less than six supper rooms—overflowing with a dizzying number of dishes. *Ragoût de veau? Gateau mille-feuille?* Meringues and blancmange baskets of fruit she recognized but the rest? Overwhelmed as she was, she had little appetite.

Again, her eyes roved the rooms she walked through, drawing attention wherever she went. Was it her gown? The intrigue of her presence? Before she could ponder it further she was blocked by a gentleman in a black half-mask dressed as a buccaneer, cutlass and all.

"*Mademoiselle* …" He bowed low, sweeping his wide-brimmed hat to one side, its ostrich feather plumes brushing the polished floor.

Onlookers encircled them as if he was more prince than pirate. When he straightened, he took her gloved hand and kissed it to the titters of more than a few fan-fluttering ladies. Next she knew they were dancing, he having returned her to the ballroom.

At midnight the music quieted for the unmasking. Though the mysterious buccaneer was still by her side, Brielle hadn't stopped looking for Bleu. Finally the *maître des cérémonies* brought the room to a standstill and then, at the trill of a violin, every mask came off, laughter and talk punctuating the dramatic moment. Brielle's *masque* dangled from her hand as she looked to Grandfather who had removed his though surely all knew the identity of their host.

He took her hand with a proud smile, his voice carrying as he introduced her. More murmuring ensued, even applause and a gasp or two, and the musicians struck the next dance. The hour she'd waited for had arrived and she needn't search any longer. Her beloved Bleu did not disappoint. Wearing a simple domino—a black silk cloak—over his suit, he walked toward her as the floor cleared for dancing. Her heart gave an answering leap at his brief, flawless bow and she curtsied, unable to mask her elation.

Bleu felt a pride he couldn't own watching Brielle. She stood out unsullied in a sea of garishness and glitter. Tonight he lost his heart to her all over again. As the excitement of the unmasking passed, she looked at him as if their last dance had been on her mind from the first. The buccaneer who'd been shadowing her finally stepped aside though he remained aggravatingly hawk-eyed.

Their dancing master had served them well. Neither of them misstepped even with so many onlookers. Years of being on the run had made him lithe on his feet though so many small, mincing dance steps didn't come naturally. He faced these new and unusual challenges for Brielle's sake. He wouldn't leave her with any regrets, just the satisfaction he had done his best in even the smallest matters.

As the dancing continued his own restlessness mounted, but finally relief came as the first guests began to depart. Done with the *fête*, he exited out a side door and up to his second-floor rooms while Brielle remained below with her grandfather and their extended relatives and lingering guests. He wasn't tired enough to sleep so he undressed to his shirt and breeches, exchanging small talk with a footman who brought him coffee. Sitting down at the desk beneath a window, he leaned back in the leather chair and watched the sunrise spill over the Loire like molten gold before gilding the shadowed gardens and terraces.

Stifling a yawn, he poured himself another *café* then inked a quill to write his sister. How did one put into words all that they were experiencing?

> *Dear Sylvie,*
>
> *It is now November, and I am considering leaving the Loire Valley after Noël. Nadine is ready to return to the Rivanna now but is willing to wait till then. Her uncle is interested in sailing to Virginia with her. As for Brielle, I do not know what her future holds. She seems happy here despite it being strange to her. Reuniting with her grandfather and other family members has gone well, better than I had hoped. The count is very hospitable despite our unexpected arrival. He asked if she plans to travel across the channel to England next to meet her father's family. For now, it is enough that she has seen France, she says.*
>
> *I am well though at sea amid so much grandeur. The count has warned us away from the intrigues and seductions of the royal courtiers at Versailles, though he has offered us his Paris townhouse. Why anyone would exchange the Loire for the city seems a poor trade. At least here there is room to roam and ride, though the valley is a far cry from the wilderness I know best.*
>
> *Forgive my poor handwriting. Last night we took part in a masked ball and I have just returned to my suite which is the size of my house. For a few days I became lost in this maze of excess. A valet has been assigned me and though I am grateful I am more inclined to trip over him than make use of him. Enough about this pleasure palace.*

Despite all the distractions and delights of France, I think of you and the children, my namesake especially, and the settlement often. I trust all of you are well. I can almost hear you asking me my plans, if I will return to my former work once I arrive. Perhaps it is wisest to return to Canada, not on Sabine's mission, but alone in search of our brothers. We might finally be at rest once we know if they have joined the Mi'kmaq or Maliseet—or have perished as we heard.

Heavy-hearted, he set the quill aside. A headache thudded at his temples likely on account of too much punch and society. Another glance out the window told him guests were still roaming the gardens. He could hear the clatter of coaches on the drive. Some even came by boat, a few of which were leaving the long landing now. He passed a hand over his eyes and leaned forward as Brielle came into view below.

Brielle ... and the buccaneer?

His gut twisted though they were not alone but in company. Even the *comte* trailed them to the water where another boat waited. The attentive Frenchman seemed to have escorted two ladies costumed as a Roman empress and a milk maid. Bleu felt another wrench as he bent over Brielle's hand in farewell. He didn't breathe any easier till the man boarded and left the land-ing—and left him wishing the boat would sink.

His dark mood shifted when Brielle returned alone from the river and looked up as if searching for him in the windows of the rooms she knew he occupied. Rising from his chair, he passed in front of the desk and stood framed by heavy brocade drapes as he looked down at her.

Pausing on the garden path amidst a tapestry of blooms, she blew him a kiss, her fingers flicking the air as if sending her heart to him instead. In that moment the rest of the world fell away, and there was only the two of them caught up in a distant dance of affection. The warmth he felt was undercut by searing longing.

She was his ... yet she wasn't.

Their shifting circumstances were carving an ever-widening chasm. He teetered on a loss like no other, even greater than Acadie, from which he'd never recover.

Exhausted and exhilarated, Brielle returned to her suite when what she wanted was to go to Bleu and tell him Grandfather's surprising news. But Bleu was in another wing of the château entirely. The kiss she'd sent him from the garden revealed the state of her heart. A rather frivolous gesture to tether them as people and events pushed them apart, even dimming the memories she had of the Rivanna, a poor relation of the River Loire, Bleu had said.

Cosette hurried to and fro as all Brielle's many layers collapsed in a heap, including the shoes that pinched her swollen feet. Mask discarded, her jewelry returned to her dressing table's jewelry box. Once the maid left, she sank to her chin in the full copper bathtub, breathing in the steaming scent of rosemary and mint. At last complete quiet reigned, though the tumult in her head and heart continued.

Of all the memories she'd made this night, one dance rose above the rest to glitter with special significance. No one, from the *fête's* beginning to end, equaled Bleu. While many men had been charming and the buccaneer in particular had paid her too much attention, she wasn't swayed in the slightest by his being a French *marquis*. And she doubted any of these nobles would be so attentive if she were to whisk off her gloves and reveal her callused hands.

Though she cared for her grandfather and was thankful for his hospitality, she continued to feel disenchanted. She'd come here willingly enough without realizing all the consequences and implications. She had merely thought to get to know her kin, not as nobility but family. Mostly she had wanted to please Bleu who felt family and home so important, too. But none of it changed her mind about her future and what she hoped for along the Rivanna River.

Unless heaven alone changed her mind and altered her course.

29

The next day Grandfather had business in Montsoreau. Brielle rose late, chiding herself for her laziness, only to find Bleu missing. Had they gone away together?

"*Non*, Mademoiselle," the steward told her. "Monsieur Galant is occupied with the grape harvest."

France's vineyards seemed to hold an ongoing fascination for him. Was he missing the Rivanna's change of seasons so this sufficed? Sorry she hadn't accompanied him, she supposed she would hear about it secondhand.

Here there were so many distractions that kept them apart. Though autumn was waning, fair weather continued, ideal for riding or being outdoors. And now that the masked ball had concluded, invitations were arriving for soirées and *veillées* and other seasonal entertainments, the social calendar full into the new year.

Would they still be here?

Grandfather seemed to take it as a matter of course. Lately when he spoke of the future it was with the certainty that she'd never leave. As if her coming here closed a door and left her no room for anything else. Had she given him that impression? Had Bleu?

Restless, she went out into the gardens she now knew by heart, seeking the landing. Early afternoon, she took a seat on a stone bench by the *château's* water gate, watching the glide of passenger boats, barges, and fishermen in both directions. Likely Bleu had taken a bateau that ferried between towns and villages. Heaven only knew when he'd return.

Today, empty of engagements, allowed her to sit in a puddle of sunlight, her hat shading her features, her ungloved hands in her lap. Her thoughts returned her to late summer when they'd left Virginia and how lush the harvest had been, how blue the river beneath a cloudless sky. Was Titus still busy with the ferry and horses? Did he miss them?

Time ticked on, the sun slanting west. Her patience was soon rewarded as she looked downriver, spying a bateau with Bleu at the bow, speaking with a *batelier*. Once docked, he jumped onto the landing and the boat resumed its watery journey, leaving them alone.

Gloriously alone.

She turned toward him on her bench seat, the unfeigned joy on his face bringing her to her feet and nearly into his arms. Removing his hat, he took her hand, brushing his lips against the back of her fingers as they stood there by the river in a moment of perfect peace and privacy.

He lapsed into English. "You look ... happy."

"Happy to see you."

"*Non*, before that. You were smiling as you sat there."

Was she? "If I close my eyes I can pretend I'm by the Rivanna instead."

"You're still dreaming of Virginia."

"I think of it often." Somehow he and Virginia had become fiercely intertwined. "And I've finally, after much thought, decided on what to call your house."

She had his full attention. "A name?"

"*Oui* ... Belle Rive."

"Beautiful shore?" His obvious pleasure doubled her own.

"Orchard Rest isn't the only handsome house along the Rivanna."

"Belle Rive it is, then." He glanced at a passing *toue* full of passengers. "Nadine sent a message yesterday saying she is growing weary of Nantes."

"So she'll return to Virginia?"

"In time," he replied vaguely.

"Grandfather said the grape harvest is nearly at an end."

"*La vendange, oui.*" His Acadian patois was becoming more classically French the longer they stayed. "The wine has been barreled and will now age before it's fit to drink."

"Do you plan to plant vineyards on those hills of yours back home?"

He chuckled. "Wine will never replace tobacco as king in the colonies. And if I stay here much longer I'm in danger of becoming a sot."

"Oh? You imbibe far less than the usual Frenchman." She'd noted his restraint with pride. "Not even champagne compares to Virginia cider."

"Agreed." He led her through the gate past the sentry and into the gardens. "Your grandfather has offered Brittany or Normandy cider from the cellars here."

"Let's try some, then."

Their orangerie doors were open, the table they'd last sat at waiting. The château was as finely tuned as a clock. Once seated a footman appeared to bring the requested cider—and a tray of other delicacies too. But Brielle's mind wasn't on the food or even the coveted cider.

Just Bleu.

Bleu took a long drink, savoring the richness of France's best apples, the tang equal to Virginia if not Acadie. "Centuries old *cidre de pomme.*"

Brielle studied him as if noticing the slight lament in his tone. "I think you're missing cidermaking on the Rivanna."

He nodded. "Acadians have a special tie to their orchards."

"Sylvie and Will wed in an apple orchard, *non?*"

"An orchard in full bloom." Even years later the memory stayed vivid. "Spring ... late May."

Brielle looked to her empty cup and held it out to him. "I wish I could have been there, too."

He poured her more. "She's teased me about doing the same ever since."

She looked up and held his gaze. As if she knew she was his every thought. As if she discerned his overwhelming feelings for her. He was having a harder time trying to hide it.

She looked away so wistfully his heart wrenched. "Grandfather has asked me to stay."

The cider's sweetness soured. "I thought he might."

"He's aging. Lonely. I'm all he has, his last link to my mother. He wants to see me marry and enjoy his grandchildren in the time left to him. He wants the *château* and all the land on the Loire to be mine—even his Paris townhouse and property should I wish it."

It was more than he'd expected—and more than she had, clearly.

"All this makes me beholden to him. How can I say no?"

It was all he could do to keep silent and not sway her decision. Their looming separation carved such a hole inside him it defied speech, yet hadn't this been his intent? To reunite her with her family and let things play out?

She pushed a strand of hair behind one pearl-studded ear. "And the marquis has asked to court me."

His composure shattered. "The buccaneer?"

She nodded, resigned. "*Le marquis de Chevreuse.*"

A nobleman, not merely a masked guest. "Do you want to be courted?"

She hesitated. Confusion crossed her face—and a rare exasperation. She held his gaze so entreatingly she seemed to be asking him to make decisions for her. "I feel ... perplexed. Taken aback."

His own perplexity reared its head. He looked away from her to see the *comte* emerging from his private barge onto the landing. He raised a hand in greeting, making straight for the orangerie.

Brielle watched his approach, still pensive. "I told him I would give him an answer after *Noël*. After I spoke with you."

"There's still time to weigh all of this," he said quietly. "For now, let's make our being here memorable."

The next night the Verdigris Salon rattled with dice and the shuffling of cards. A great many guests gathered to enjoy a rainy evening of games as the weather turned chill. Autumn seemed to have fled taking all lightheartedness and beauty with it. In some inexplicable way Brielle felt cheated, confined to a gilded cage that kept her from what she truly wanted.

What was winter like along the Rivanna?

She sat near the flickering hearth, playing *jeu de l'oie* with several ladies. She'd never been one for games though whist, trictrac, marelle, piquet and lansquenet played out all around her. Betting began and gold and silver coins crossed half a dozen tables like bon-bons. Oddly, it brought back the *Rose and Crown* and all its dark memories. Though far more refined than a tavern, the sounds and smells seemed the same—ceaseless laughter, chatter, spirits, and tobacco smoke.

Bleu sat at the table nearest her, teaching Grandfather and the *marquis* and another man how to play Waltes. He'd packed the Mi'kmaq game in his luggage which had become something of a favorite among captain and crew on the voyage here. The decorated ivory dice, cup, and wooden counting sticks seemed more art, returning her to his Canadian heritage—and Sabine Broussard.

Had she made it safely to Acadie?

Paying little attention to her own game, Brielle watched Bleu under lowered lashes, tracing all the beloved contours of him, his profile so striking in the candlelight her stomach swirled. Occasionally he would look up and meet her eyes though he seemed wholly immersed in the game.

Sometimes *le marquis de Chevreuse* would turn his dark, heavy gaze on her. As the evening wore on his playing seemed more personal. He, at least, seemed intent on impressing her. Grandfather's back was to her as he helped with counting and scoring, his pleasure palpable that all seemed to be genuinely enjoying the game.

"And the prize, gentlemen?" Madame Bellamy asked from another table as she moved her token forward on the board. "We are playing for a jade broach. And you?"

Bleu paused from rolling dice as Chevreuse shrugged narrow shoulders. "*Un baiser?*"

A kiss?

The *marquis* winked, his intensity shifting as his gaze slid from Madame Bellamy to Brielle. Her stomach tightened as she returned to her own game and tried to focus to no avail. A quarter of an hour ticked past—nearly midnight—and dice were still rattling, scores tallying.

She'd never been kissed.

And kissing the marquis was not what she wanted. To equate such intimacy with something as trivial as a game prize left her half ill. Kisses weren't made for crowded, smoky, wine-sated rooms but private places. Let him kiss someone else if he won.

Her heart was wholly taken.

"A kiss?" Madame Bellamy eyed Chevreuse shrewdly. "From which lady, *monsieur le marquis?*" When he didn't answer she continued, "Not *Mademoiselle* Farrow, surely, since you must first get past her *ange gardien.*"

Low laugher filled the room and Brielle had to smile.

So, they thought Bleu her guardian angel?

As for the ladies *jeu de l'oie,* Madame Bellamy soon won the broach and they disbanded for refreshments before returning to watch Waltes. The unusual game continued tensely, Bleu and the marquis so focused it seemed they weren't aware they were surrounded. As the wooden platter of dice came down a final time with enough force to rattle and rearrange them, Bleu leaned back in his chair as the *comte* declared the winner.

"Monsieur Galant, *vous avez triomphé!*"

A titter erupted from the ladies. Brielle clapped, unsurprised yet pleased Bleu had won and by doing so removed her from the unwelcome attentions of another man. The *marquis's* smile was thin as Bleu rose from the table without a word and went to a sideboard where he poured champagne into an engraved glass before a footman could do so.

"Will you not claim your prize, Monsieur Galant?" Chevreuse asked, his words more taunt as his gaze returned to Brielle.

"A kiss is not a trifling thing given as some offhand, haphazard prize." Bleu turned back around and faced him. "It is from the heart. Sacred. To be expressed in secret."

For a telling second his eyes met Brielle's and her heart held still.

Had he ever kissed a woman? Might she be the very first?

Madame Janvier looked at him admiringly. "For all your *férocité*, Monsieur Galant, you are a true *romantique* at heart."

Another round of games began. Bleu sat down with Grandfather to play chess while Chevreuse joined several other gentlemen at piquet. Hiding a yawn behind her extended fan, Brielle went to a near window, wishing an end to the evening. She took a deep breath, her pulse hardly settling. Bleu's heartfelt words wooed her as only he could do. They were of the same mind about intimate matters as well as the mundane.

At last the clock struck two and the company traded the salon for the terrace, walking toward the landing where their transport waited. Soon winter would force them to their carriages and river traffic would dwindle.

Brielle walked with the ladies to the river, torches illuminating their path. Uncomfortably aware of the marquis, she stood by the water gate as their guests boarded the boats to depart.

"I wish, *Mademoiselle*, to show you *Château d'Ussé*," Chevreuse told her. "Especially my renowned grottoes given your penchant for gardens."

She managed to smile, not wanting to encourage him nor be rude. Though Grandfather had told her Chevreuse wanted to court her he hadn't shared his own feelings about the matter. Nor had she expressed hers. So much about French etiquette eluded her—courting customs foremost.

"Say you'll come upriver so that I can give you a tour," he told her.

He was standing so close she took a sudden step back. The last boat had departed, all but Chevreuse's at the end of the landing, a poleman snoring in the bow. Alarm jarred her at being alone with him. Grandfather had been here a moment ago but now no one else stood in the shadows but the two of them. Surely it wasn't sensible to tarry with so inebriated and enamored a man—

"Ah, a private moment at last. You've been such a temptation to me all evening—your lovely gown, the enchanting way you talk with your hands and move about a room." His fingers encircled her wrist like a bracelet. "You play the flirt even if you don't mean to ..."

He continued murmuring, his impassioned French eluding her. She caught only the barest, most alarming words. *Temptation. Coquette. Desire.* His wine-soured breath made her recoil.

"Pardon, *monsieur* ..." She started toward the *château*, trying to pull free. "I must return to the house *now.*"

"Not until we are finished here." He pulled her against him with both hands, the buttons of his frock coat pressing into her bodice and the soft, exposed skin above it. "Say you'll come upriver—"

His slurred words ended as he was knocked backwards with such force Brielle felt the blow. Her arm felt wrenched from its socket as the *marquis* let her go. He stumbled only to be hit again as Bleu shoved him further from Brielle and off the landing. The river's splash wet her skirts as she whirled and faced Bleu, the hard lines of his face terrifying by torch light. She'd never seen him so livid.

The poleman, now wide awake, held out an oar to the *marquis* who flailed about like a drowning river rat. With a last, dismissive glance, Bleu took her arm as gently as the marquis had been harsh and escorted her from the landing and back to the *château*.

She wanted to kiss him then and there.

30

The next morning, Brielle came downstairs to find a black-coated gentlemen leaving Grandfather's study. He passed without a glance at her, following a footman to the main entrance. Finding the study door closed, she knocked lightly.

"*Entrez.*"

Bleu stood with Grandfather by the hearth. Rarely did she venture here, preferring the salon with her mother's portrait or the library or her own suite. Rain spackled the windowpanes, ushering in a deeper chill that seemed to announce winter was at hand—and *Noël*. Though she wanted to see how the French celebrated Christmas, she most wanted Christmas along the Rivanna River. An Acadian celebration.

"*Bonjour, mes chers messieurs,*" she said with a smile as Grandfather motioned her inside the mahogany-paneled room.

Bleu met her eyes, no doubt thinking of last night's riverside debacle, too. In hindsight, she found the memory comical. The blow backwards—the river's satisfying splash—the frantic pole-man who'd had to fish the humbled *marquis* out of the water.

But no one seemed to be smiling now.

"Have I missed something?" she asked, looking from one to the other. "I just saw someone leaving ..."

"*Comte de Villeneuve.*" Grandfather motioned to the settee that fronted the hearth. "An unwelcome guest, I'm afraid."

Bleu stood to one side of the robust fire, hands clasped behind his back. He looked as calm as he'd been furious last night, in stark contrast to Grandfather who appeared unusually ruffled. Settling on the sofa, Brielle smoothed her petticoats, waiting for one of them to elaborate.

"Not all Frenchmen, even noblemen, behave as gentlemen as you found out last night," Grandfather began, taking a seat beside her. "Chevreuse is more arrogant than gallant. The man you saw leaving my study is his second who, in his stead, has formally issued a challenge to Monsieur Galant to defend his honor which was somewhat dampened by being thrown into the river."

"A challenge?" Brielle wanted to scoff. "For defending *my* honor from his rude, ungentlemanly conduct of last night?"

Grandfather frowned. "*Oui,* a duel."

Brielle looked at Bleu, warmed by his defense of her by the river, believing it bespoke his feelings for her. "You didn't accept."

He lifted his shoulders. "I ... delayed."

"Dueling is illegal but proud nobles still persist." Grandfather shook his head in disgust. "There is nothing so foolish in North America, neither Canada nor the colonies, to my knowledge."

"People are too busy trying to stay alive—survive—than endanger themselves with ridiculous dueling." Brielle spoke so vehemently Bleu regarded her with surprise, even a new tenderness.

Was he remembering her tavern days? How fearful she'd been? How hungry at times?

"Now seems a good time to say I want nothing more to do with the *marquis* nor have I ever wanted him to court me," she finished.

"There are others ..." Grandfather left off.

Bleu's wry half-smile seemed to say *I told you so* as Grandfather continued.

"You have several admirers, those who are waiting in the wings, so to speak, but ..."

But Bleu.

She knew the gist of his thoughts without his finishing. Bleu was enough of a presence to deter even the most ardent suitors. What had Madame Bellamy called him?

Ton ange gardien?

If not for Bleu, she might have been harmed by the foppish Chevreuse who'd been so staggeringly drunk. And now he had sent his second with a ridiculous challenge that had nothing to do with her but his wounded pride and rather public humiliation.

Perhaps now was the time for them to return home. Though the Rivanna River settlement hadn't been hers for long, the memories too few, it still felt like home, every thought of it embroidered with longing.

"So what does this dueling entail?" Bleu asked as the corner clock struck eleven and she remembered she had a pressing engagement.

"If you accept the challenge, you must select a second then choose your weapons." Grandfather looked to the hearth as the fire popped and showered the marble tiles with sparks. "Duels are often conducted at dawn in secret locations to elude the authorities. Your seconds and a surgeon would accompany you. Ground rules would be laid."

Brielle's ire overrode her usual composure. "Ground rules for idiocy that has been outlawed?"

"Sheer idiocy, *oui*. Nevertheless, the duel must be conducted honorably, no matter how dishonorably it began," he explained, his expression darkening. "You begin by saluting your opponent then take your positions. The fight might be quick or prolonged, the first to draw blood the victor."

Brielle looked hard at him as if it could curb this complication. As for Bleu, he continued to regard her grandfather stoically, even calmly, as if they were only discussing foul weather.

"I wonder which weapons Chevreuse prefers," Bleu murmured.

"It matters not whether he prefers pistols or rapiers, *Monsieur* Galant," he replied. "You are twice the man he is. I fear you will kill him."

His chilling tone gave her pause. Long ago Bleu had nearly killed Sylvie's future husband—an enemy soldier—in Acadie. The details were unknown to her, but she'd always sensed something feral about Bleu despite his surface civility. She'd witnessed only a fraction of that by the river last night.

Perhaps Bleu should leave, not because she feared for his safety, but because he was free to come and go as he pleased. He had no ties to France. French codes of honor didn't apply to a man who was from another continent, his own moral codes so far above Chevreuse the entire matter was ludicrous, even laughable. She believed the *marquis* was as avaricious as he was a rake. Perhaps he suspected Grandfather was poised to leave everything to her which surely spurred his pursuit.

"Chevreuse is a fool," she said quietly but with disgust, resisting the urge to roll her eyes. That was the effect the French fop had on her. And she felt wildly and irrationally protective of Bleu who was more than capable of fending for himself.

A footman appeared at the door and for a moment she feared the foolish second had returned. "Your carriage waits, *Mademoiselle*."

Bleu looked at her in question.

"I'm to have tea at the Pavillon downriver," she said, wishing otherwise. Sometimes society was too much. And to leave with this matter in limbo ...

"Wear a warm wrap, *petite fille*, as the day is cooler than yesterday," Grandfather cautioned. "Those clouds moving in from the west portend a storm. If the weather turns inclement it would be wise for you to stay on at the Pavillon."

She kissed him farewell, not making any promises. She wanted to do the same with Bleu as she looked back from the doorway and met his gaze. Such a long look he gave her, as if he was memorizing every detail of her with a quiet intensity that held unspoken devotion. If love could be communicated in a look ...

Had he communicated his here and now?

Downriver, Brielle sat amongst the other *demoiselles* in their brightly colored dresses to enjoy conversation, tea, and hot chocolate. The Pavillon was a small manor house owned by their countess hostess. Lovely as her circumstances and company were, Brielle was having a hard time following their effusive, rapid French, her thoughts returning to Bleu. Away from him, she merely seemed to be biding her time till she saw him next.

"And you, Gabrielle ..." Her hostess turned toward her. "What will you wear to the duchess's winter *fête*? Your gown at the masked ball was *ravissante*!"

Thunder nearly overrode her answer as the young ladies flew to the salon's windows to watch the storm Grandfather had predicted. Brielle stayed seated as lightning lit the afternoon darkness in brilliant flashes, rain slanting down in silver sheets beyond the glass.

The storm outside mirrored the tumult inside her. How would this matter with Chevreuse end? A dozen different outcomes played in her mind but Bleu's last look at her stayed uppermost. Odd how easily she forgot exchanges with others but not a word with him. There always seemed to be an undercurrent of something more between them, albeit unspoken, a feeling too deep for words. She felt it hours—days—after and missed him with every speck of her being.

Sitting here in this frivolous room making frivolous conversation when someone she disdained had the temerity to call him out seemed a punishment. Yet here she sat, unable to return to the *château* because the coach's horses couldn't be risked in the storm. She could only sit and pray for a way out of their present predicament including an end to the storm within and without.

31

*H*e wouldn't come between an old man and his only granddaughter. That was the crux of the matter. In his suite, Bleu pondered what he'd told the *comte* before he'd left his study earlier this morning.

I have overstayed my welcome, Monsieur. Remaining here would cause a scandal for you and your granddaughter which is not my intent. It has become apparent no man will approach her—court her—so long as I am present. A ship is leaving Nantes for Virginia soon. I'll return to port as soon as the weather clears if you'll kindly loan me a coach.

He packed his trunk, his relief at returning to North America at odds with his devotion to Brielle. But he had completed what he'd hoped for by reuniting her with her grandfather. She had the whole world before her, a far brighter future than any he could offer in America or elsewhere. Once on board ship there would be plenty of time to decide his own future. He might well go to Acadie if only to clear his heart and head of her. If he ever could.

For now, he packed and welcomed being preoccupied with the coming journey since it left him little time to dwell on her. Midafternoon the thunder and lightning cleared though rain continued to pelt down. Traveling so late in the year was hazardous, and he needed to determine if Nadine was ready to go suddenly or if he'd sail alone provided he found passage. Sailings were fewer in winter, the seas more dangerous.

Brielle would be unhappy with his leaving, as unhappy as he himself was, and so a letter would spare them both a final, wrenching goodbye. Taking out ink and paper left him unusually choked and groping for words. In an agony of remorse, he filled one page, then two. He'd prayed for the right time, the right words—had the Almighty provided that by keeping Brielle at the Pavillon?

He'd leave her with the one thing he had left from Acadie, a final, heartfelt gift that could be worn this winter. He valued it like he had the Lyonnaise silk he'd brought Sylvie long ago, never thinking Brielle would wear it, too. Removing the fur from his trunk, he left it by his letter.

The few miles to Nantes passed in a blur. He was strangely weary as if all his carefully stowed feelings since he'd first found Brielle at the crossroads were taking an inward toll. By the time the lights of Nantes came into view his spirits had sunk to his boots. But he pressed on, hauling his trunk into the inn, securing the same room he'd had before, and sending a message to the docks about departing ships. He wouldn't chance going himself. After dark, thieves, smugglers, and pirates flooded the taverns along the harbor where drunkenness and disorder ruled.

He went downstairs to the dining room, realizing he'd not eaten supper, the rumble in his gut no match for the hollowness in his heart. Midnight brought a reply. *L'Aimable* would sail with the tide. Felicitous timing, that. He consulted tide tables pinned to the wall near the inn's entrance and awaited a reply from Nadine. At last it came. She would sail with him accompanied by her uncle and promised to arrive in the morning.

All was falling into place.

Bleu lay down in his lodgings as the inn's noise faded to a few footsteps and an occasional slammed door. The public rooms were on the ground floor at the other end of the building, sparing him the fumes of spirits and smoke. Weary as he was, he couldn't sleep. Questions spun through his head as the ache inside him widened.

He hadn't known such misery since his family had been forced from Acadie and he'd stood on shore and watched the rotting transports depart and the British set fire to Acadie's homesteads. Tonight he seemed to be coming apart all over again as another sort of anguish tore at him, made up of unmet, unrealized needs and abandoned dreams and all that he'd left unspoken.

Dieu, aide-moi.

Had he not given this matter over to the Almighty? Surrendered Brielle to Him and asked Him to cover her if he could not? Only sheer will kept him from returning to the *château*. This devilish lack of peace gave him no rest.

At last Brielle left the Pavillon and arrived back at the château to find Grandfather looking strangely dejected. She kissed both his cheeks, and he embraced her a bit longer than usual, raising her alarm.

"Are you well?" she asked worriedly as a servant took her wraps.

"I'm relieved you've returned safely." He led her into the adjoining salon. "But it is always melancholy when a beloved guest departs. As of yesterday, Monsieur Galant has left."

"Left? In such stormy weather?" The bottom dropped out of her stomach. "What do you mean?"

"He has gone to Nantes and is preparing to sail to Virginia if he hasn't done so already. He left you a letter—"

"*Grand-père!*" Her voice broke. She looked frantically at the clock as if she could stop its ticking. "Why did you not talk him out of it?"

"*Ma chère* ..." His aged face had never looked so sorrowful. "He thought it wise to go for many reasons and I could not prevent him."

Rushing from the room, she hardly heard him, a sick panic shadowing her as she sought the staircase to Bleu's rooms. Where had he left the letter?

Why had he left *her*?

Suddenly an entire ocean separating them seemed a chasm too deep. If he'd truly gone—if she couldn't reach him in time ...

She burst into his empty suite as if her haste could somehow help the situation. His treasured scent threaded the air though the room was empty of all his belongings. There on his desk lay an open, unsealed letter—and a black sable muff and cape, the fur so glossy it shone like onyx. Had it come from Canada? Of his own making?

She lifted the letter, her tears spattering the black ink. She let them fall, not wanting to take the time to dig for a handkerchief. His slanted letters reminded her he was left-handed. Writing, he'd said, had never been his forte.

Ma belle Brielle ...
My beautiful Brielle. Her crushed heart seemed to stop.
This is not how I wanted to say goodbye, but I doubt I would be able to leave you in person so this must suffice. Please accept this gift of my hands and heart, a black sable muff and cape from my beloved Acadie instead of the miniature you wanted painted of me.

Accompanying you to France has been the greatest joy of my life. Non, it began before that, when I first found you at the inn in the foothills. I knew even then you were made for finer things. I had never seen so lovely and gracious a woman, a true beauty, nor one more deserving of regaining all you have lost.

Now that I have played a small part in reuniting you with your grandfather I can go more easily, if not let go easily. There are a thousand things I would rather say than farewell, but life is far from a fairytale no matter how much we wish it. Au revoir.

For now and always, I remain your ever devoted
—Bleu

When dawn broke after a near sleepless night, Bleu was already on his feet and dressed, shouldering his trunk as he went below. The gifts he and Brielle had chosen for Sylvie and her family waited in another large trunk in the inn's foyer.

Nadine and her uncle were at the entrance, their own baggage in a hand cart. Upon loading his own, the three of them left the inn together after exchanging a terse greeting. Yesterday's stormy weather had vanished. The clear if cold day failed to lift his spirits though it made for fine sailing.

"Where is Brielle?" Nadine asked, the question arrow sharp.

"She'll remain in France with her grandfather," he replied, keeping his eyes on the sun as it poured over a confusion of warehouses and shops and quays. Vessels of all shapes and sizes— merchantmen, frigates, brigs, corsairs, even the nightmarish slave ships—and a host of scents, not all of them savory, assailed them as orders were shouted in French and Breton and languages he'd never heard.

L'Amiable's captain greeted them and recorded their names on the manifest as a cabin boy came to collect their baggage. A three-masted merchantman, its square linen sails taut in the wind, the ship bore a small number of cannons mounted on the upper deck, a figurehead and decorative elements on the stern marking the ship's home port.

The tide was rushing in, swelling the activity in the harbor as ships readied to weigh anchor. While Nadine and her uncle went below deck, Bleu watched sailors climb the rigging and all deck-hands make ready to depart. Bound for French-held *Louisiane*, the vessel would first dock in Virginia—York Town—before making its way along the coast further south.

He stood by the railing and faced the immensity of the ocean, back turned on Nantes as the wintry wind beat at him and frothed the water into a restless rhythm. They weighed anchor earlier than planned, the creak of the vessel pronounced as it left its moorings. His heart, torn and now broken, seemed to plummet to the harbor's bottom.

32

At full speed, Grandfather's carriage rivaled Brielle's racing heart. Wrapped in the cape Bleu had given her, she stroked the sable muff absently, wishing the soft fur was his warm arms. When the walls and spires of Nantes came into view, she prayed as she'd never prayed before for some delay. She refused to think his goodbye meant she had no hold on his heart.

Grandfather sat across from her, clutching his silver-headed cane, largely silent as if fully occupied with weathering every bump and bend in the road. She hadn't reckoned on how hard this would be for him. Sympathy pierced her panic, turning her mouth dry and scattering her thoughts as they veered round another precarious corner.

Was this not simply another valley in the landscape of her life?

She'd endured much since her parents died. A loss of home and personal liberty. Servitude through indenture. The lewd looks of men and the envy of women. A future fraught with uncertainty. But nothing seared her quite like this. She was so rattled she was having trouble drawing an easy breath. By the time they'd reached *The White Cross,* their elegant, pristine vehicle was more mud than burgundy paint.

"Allow me to go inside and inquire, *chère Gabrielle,*" Grandfather said once they'd rolled to a stop.

Nodding, she leaned into the coach's open window, searching every face, every form on the busy street for sign of Bleu or Nadine. Grandfather returned quickly, simply telling the coachman to hasten to the harbor where he again left the coach to disappear inside a large stone structure facing the water. The *capitaine de port*? Such a maze of quays and docks and ships even late in the season.

A sleek merchantman was leaving now, slipping from its moorings and her line of sight. A flash of scarlet on its broad deck caught her eye. *Nadine?* Brielle knew that fringed shawl anywhere. Nadine stood along the railing beside a short, hatless man. Not Bleu.

Where was he?

Turning away from the coach window, she fumbled with the door's latch. In her haste she nearly tripped on the step onto muddy cobbles. Clutching her silk skirts, she began to run, her voice carrying over the water. "Nadine!"

The large ship was moving, slowly gaining speed. Brielle dismissed Nadine as well as sailors and passengers alike in her frantic search. Her heart seized when she spied a tall figure at the stern. Bleu stood alone, facing forward and away from her, his dark coattails fluttering in the wind.

Her voice rose then broke. "Bleu!"

She ran faster, dodging sailors and cargo and all else. The long wooden quay seemed to shake beneath her feet as it stretched into the churlish water. She shouted over and over till her words became a hoarse cry.

Still, he didn't turn around. How could he hear her with so many screeching gulls and the wind off the water? She reached the end of the quay in utter defeat.

As *L'Amiable* picked up speed, Bleu saw Nadine hurrying toward him, her features scored with alarm.

"Bleu! *Regarde vers rivage!*"

Look toward shore.

Confused, he turned, the wind pressing against him as if determined to turn him around again. Another gust snatched his cocked hat from his head and sent it over the railing as his gaze swept the waterfront.

Brielle?

She was at the end of a quay—had she fallen? On her knees, head in her hands, her petticoats in a heap around her. And she wore his sable cape, the muff beside her. Even at a distance her emotion struck him hard. *Anguished.* As anguished as he was.

"Brielle!" The cold wind flung his shout away.

Her head remained in her hands, her shoulders shaking. Only a woman in love would make such a vulnerable public display. Though he knew his going would upset her, he assumed she would move past it and come to realize France had far more to offer. But her heart had clearly broken.

He had broken it.

Seconds passed before his head caught up with *his* heart and made sense of the matter. He removed his frock coat, his measured movements belying the rising tick of his pulse. His shoes and stockings came next before he hoisted himself atop the taffrail and faced into the wind. The jacks on deck—and Nadine—watched in a sort of horrorstruck awe as the ship continued its slow, powerful pull from port.

Poised to jump, Bleu's mind spun backwards to the moonlit night he'd fought William Blackburn on the *Constellation's* quarterdeck before he dove into *Baie Française.* Then and now, he sprang like a mink off the rail. Twenty feet down he met saltwater, the waves and ripples of the ship's wake closing over him in a white, bubbling rush. Acadie's waters had been colder.

He fought his way to the surface, Brielle firmly in mind. His sure, swift strokes cut through the briny foam, bringing him nearer the quay. He stayed clear of departing vessels, the shore becoming more distinct, the cry of the gulls and dockside shouts ringing in his ears. Brielle still sat, head in her hands, as if unable to watch *L'Amiable's* leaving.

Would she not look up?

As the wind freshened and blew cold off the water, a Scripture Brielle knew by heart pierced her angst-ridden thoughts.

I found him whom my soul loveth.

But was it not to be? Had she loved Bleu wrongly? Dearly and a bit desperately, *oui*. Had he no lasting regard of her other than to reunite her with family? All she had left of him was a letter and the beautiful fur she wore.

By coming to France she'd wanted to show him that a life of affluence would not alter her feelings for him. She wanted to ensure he understood that her choice was genuine and not merely because France had been untried. *Non*, she had been there and still she'd chosen him.

Heartsick, she stared at the ship now far beyond her reach, a mere speck of wood and sail on the horizon. Strength spent, she closed her eyes against the stinging wind until a sudden splash made her open them again. Below the quay's edge was a strangely sodden figure treading water. With his black hair splayed over his head and shoulders, the man she loved hardly looked himself.

The shock of it brought her to her feet. Stepping on her muff, she scrambled to throw him the thick rope that wound round a

near piling. In her haste she stumbled, sending both herself and
the rope over the quay's edge. With a little cry she smacked the
water. The breathless plunge downward was worsened by a melee
of petticoats that acted like an anchor. In seconds his hard arms
caught her, pulling her upwards toward light and air. Choking
and sputtering, she grappled for her bearings as Bleu tied the rope
around her then began to hoist himself upwards.

In a few moments he'd gained the quay only to pull at the
rope, lifting her from the water. She collapsed atop the stones
beside him, the both of them dazed and breathless. His arms went
round her, her head against the linen shirt pasted to his chest.
Beneath her ear his heart pulsed nearly as frantically as her own.

"Now seems the time to say," he began in brief, winded bursts,
his mouth warm against her ear, "till death do us part."

"Are you asking me …?"

"With all my heart," he answered, freeing her from the rope.

They sat, nearly intertwined, till their breathing quieted and
the tumult of the moment passed. Leaning in, he kissed her, his
lips brushing hers with such intent she forgot all else. Her arms
encircled his neck and she kissed him back, the moment charged
with all the love they'd quelled, a dizzying rush of elation and passion that left her lightheaded. Only the screech of a gull overhead
ended their newfound intimacy.

Slowly, Bleu got to his feet and brought her to hers. "I want to
keep kissing you more than I want to be warm and dry, *ma mariée*."
His eyes were smiling. Had he called her his bride? "But we are
drawing attention and your grandfather is almost here."

Jubilant, they joined hands and faced the caped man walking
toward them who regarded them with a sort of bemused wonder.
"*Tourtereaux* …" *Lovebirds.* Grandfather, despite everything, looked
supremely pleased. "I hardly know what to say except that I am
not at all surprised by this turn of events."

Bleu looked down at the quay, his grin slightly sheepish as he picked up the discarded muff. "I have obviously abandoned ship, *comte*."

"A small matter." Chuckling, Grandfather leaned into his cane as the wind rocked him. "Now seems a good time to tell you that I own a vessel which will take you two wherever you wish to go."

Did he?

"Come with us to Virginia, then." Brielle lay a damp hand on his sleeve. "I want nothing more than your blessing at our wedding alongside a river very different than your Loire."

Bleu met his eyes as another blast of wind buffeted them. "You told me it has long been your wish to see the New World."

"Very well." Grandfather smiled. "I suppose I am not too old to cross an ocean."

33

Rivanna River, Virginia
March, 1765

*T*heir wedding day.

Brielle arrived at the chapel early, long before any guests or even the itinerate pastor. Someone—Sylvie?—had already been at work, decorating with ribbons and dried everlastings ahead of the ceremony. But she'd since disappeared, likely up the hill at Orchard Rest with her growing brood, the baby, especially.

For a time Brielle feared they wouldn't live to see this long-anticipated day. Their tumultuous return to Virginia had been no easier than the crossing to France but they had all survived it and now, a fortnight after finding their land legs in York Town, it was their wedding day. Even the weather was obliging. Sunlight streamed through newly washed windows, creating a lacy pattern on the plank floor. A *bon* morning.

Ahead of the wedding, Brielle had moved to the finished and newly named Belle Rive. She explored each room, finding a hundred little touches she loved from the corner fireplaces to the parlor bookshelves and the fleur-de-lis newel post in the hall. Till the wedding, Bleu stayed at Orchard Rest, turning his hand to tending the orchards and spending time with Titus along the river.

Grandfather took her place in the cottage, his joy at being surrounded by Sylvie's children a sight to behold. Even the settlement *enfants* called him *Pépère* which brought out his robust laugh and had him continually emptying his pockets of comfits and tiny toys gotten in Williamsburg.

Gratefulness at being back in the place that felt like home, mistress of a new house she hoped to fill with children, about to wed the man she'd loved from the very first, filled her with an overwhelming sense of wellbeing that made all the hardships and hurdles of the past a pinprick.

When a footfall sounded at the chapel's open doors, she turned toward it in anticipation. Bleu stepped inside and held out a hand to her. Quickly she closed the distance between them, her Lyonnaise silk rustling. Clad in a French-made suit, he looked every inch the groom she'd long imagined.

His eyes were a wash of blue. Was he thinking this moment almost never happened? That at the very last they'd nearly been separated by an ocean? If not for his boldness in jumping ship or her own frantic pursuit—

"Will you finally do me the honor of becoming Gabrielle Galant?" His emphasis on *finally* made her smile. "I knew at first meeting I would never be the same … and so here we are."

"No more of you here and me there but everything shared." She squeezed his hand. "Your table, your bed, your babies. Every sunrise and sunset from our porch."

"All of it, *oui*." He brought her fingers to his lips. "A happy but humble beginning."

"Little is needed to make a happy life."

"Love, faith, family—a firm foundation." He took her in his arms as children's excited voices sounded outside the chapel. "Ours is *une dévotion féroce*."

Epilogue

Belle Rive
Rivanna River, Virginia
May, 1772

"*L*ook, Papa, at the painted sky!"

The little girl, barely three years old, perched on the edge of a sturdy wooden chair, her bare feet dusted with the day's play. Plump legs swinging, she waited for her parents to share her view. It was a beloved ritual most evenings no matter the season. In winter they watched from the windows; warmer weather had them outside.

Bleu climbed the porch steps, his attention shifting from Brielle in the open doorway to their little daughter, a French-made doll from *Pépère* clutched close, its painted features and fancy dress worn. Watching her, his heart felt too big for his chest. A warm wind stirred the wisteria climbing the porch posts and his daughter's unruly curls. She had her mother's mahogany hair and his Acadie blue eyes—and one deeply dimpled cheek entirely her own.

Their older, twin sons were still by the river with their cousins from Orchard Rest, their shared talk and laughter heard up the hill.

Mirabel looked over her shoulder at a smiling Brielle. "The sky is sleepy, *Maman*, and nearly abed."

She stretched out her arms, her doll forgotten, as Bleu took her on his lap in the largest rattan chair. Yawning, she nestled against him as Brielle sank into the seat beside them and took his hand, the three of them overlooking the sleepy, painted sunset.

Fireflies began their slow, blinking dance against the violet-blue horizon that stretched endlessly toward the places he once roamed. But that was another, now distant life exchanged for a far richer, rooted one.

He had found home.

Author Note

I fell in love with France while there researching *The Rose and the Thistle,* never imagining I'd revisit it in Bleu Galant's story. True to Bleu, he took me on quite an adventure, a secondary character that seemed made for France, especially having found the love of his life who shares his French ancestry. When writing *The Seamstress of Acadie* I was somewhat enamored with Bleu and continued to wonder who would win him in the end. And now we know the rest of the story.

Special thanks to Jenny Q. (Quinlan) of Historical Editorial for taking a very rough draft of this novella and advising me on what worked and what didn't. She has a special magic with historical fiction that is second to none. Kudos to Shelli Littleton for her editing and proofreading excellence every single time. Her dedication and love for the written word inspires me again and again. To the very gifted Jill Kemerer, Books & Such Literary Agency, Janet Grant, and Story Architect. You make the reading world a much better, more blessed place.

And last but not least, to Mr. Michael Bernard, wherever you are. Long ago you, and Tates Creek, led me here.

Made in the USA
Coppell, TX
06 September 2025

54415835R00132